Eye

of the

Ocelot

Eye

of the

Ocelot

AN ABIGAIL FIORELLI MYSTERY

VOLTA
ROSE

GreenHeart
BOOKS

Reading, Vermont

For information about this title or to order other books and/or electronic media, contact the publisher:

Green Heart Books
Reading, Vermont USA
www.greenheartbooks.com
info@greenheartbooks.com

Botanical image: USDA, NRCS. 2022. PLANTS Database (https://plants.sc.egov.usda.gov/, 09/30/2022). National Plant Data Team, Greensboro, NC 27401-4901 USA

"The Fisherman and His Sons" is an original adaptation of a traditional selkie tale by Duncan Williamson (1928-2007) in the Scottish Traveller oral tradition. Adapted with permission from the first publication of the story in *The Broonie, Silkies and Fairies* by Duncan Williamson (Edinburgh: Canongate, 1987). Edited by Linda Williamson.

Cover and interior design by The Book Cover Whisperer:
OpenBookDesign.biz

978-0-9727518-4-1 Paperback
978-0-9727518-1-0 Hardcover
978-0-9727518-7-2 eBook

Publisher's Cataloging-in-Publication data

Names: Rose, Volta, author.
Title: Eye of the ocelot / Volta Rose.
Series: Abigail Fiorelli Mysteries
Description: Reading, VT: Green Heart Books, 2022.

Identifiers: LCCN: 2022942125 | ISBN: 978-0-9727518-1-0 (hardcover) | ISBN 978-0-9727518-4-1 (paperback) | 978-0-9727518-7-2 (epub)

Subjects: LCSH Detectives--Fiction. | Endangered species--Fiction. | Cape Cod (Mass.)--Fiction. | Mystery fiction. | Romance fiction. | BISAC FICTION / Mystery & Detective / General | FICTION / Romance / General

Classification: LCC PS3618.O793 E94 2022 | DDC 813.6--dc23

FIRST EDITION

www.GreenHeartBooks.com

GREEN HEART BOOKS and the green heart
image are registered trademarks.

She was at one with the elements,
the land and the sea.
Abigail was no less than a goddess:
Aurora calling in the dawn.

Prologue

Abby had been playing with her friends in the forest when they discovered a tree dassie. The nocturnal animal was caught out in the open in a small tree at sunrise, exposing it to danger.

"See how cute it is!" exclaimed Abby's best friend, Iragena. Abby loved Iragena's name because it had the same meaning as something her father always said: "God provides."

"Let's get closer," whispered Abby.

The young hyrax was about a foot long, and looked like a giant guinea pig.

Suddenly, Iragena's brother threw a rock at the dassie, striking it in the back. It let out a loud shriek. Abby ran over and pushed him, yelling, "Stop it, Gahigi! You're going to hurt it!"

"I am Gahigi, the hunter," he replied.

"You're going to have to hunt me first!" Abby yelled, pushing him so hard he fell onto the ground. Even though Gahigi was a full head taller than Abby, he got up sheepishly and began to back away.

"If you're so big," taunted Gahigi, "see if you can catch me!" He turned and ran back toward the village.

No matter how hard she tried, Abby was just not fast enough to catch him. By the time she reached the village and entered the door of her house, she was completely winded and promptly collapsed on the couch.

"Abby, you're just in time for lunch," called her mother. "What have you been doing? You're covered in sweat."

As they ate, Abby told her parents what had happened. "You can't save every animal in the bush," remarked her father.

"Yes, I can," Abby stubbornly insisted.

"Your Swahili name is well-earned," said her father. "That's for certain."

"They call me Mlinzi," said Abby.

"Yes, you are *Defender*," he affirmed. "Sometimes you are also Mkali."

"What does that mean?" asked Abby.

"*Fierce.*"

~

ABBY LOOKED AT HER mother and realized she had been silent ever since they'd sat down to eat. "Mommy, is something the matter?"

"Abby, I have something to share with you. It's important that you listen carefully. Don't be afraid. Everything is going to be alright." Abby knew Fiona would not say that everything was going to be alright if she wasn't concerned about something serious. The young girl put down her fork and sat up straight in her chair, looking intently into her mom's eyes.

Abby's mother tried to speak, but a lump rose in her throat, preventing the words from coming. Her father, Angelo, gently placed his hand on top of his wife's. "What your mother is trying to say, Abby, is that she is very sick."

"Mommy?" Abby implored, beginning to shake as tears welled up.

"It's true, honey," Fiona confirmed. "But you don't need to worry. There's a doctor in Boston who can help me get well."

"I don't understand, Mommy," said Abby in a quivering voice.

"Abby, we're going to need to leave Nkuli and go to Boston so I can see a special doctor and get the treatment I need." She reached out to touch Abby's hand, but her daughter pulled away. "I'm sorry, honey. It's not something any of us want, but it's what we have to do so I can get better. You're going to have to be very brave, dear. Do you think you can do that?"

Abby could hardly hear what her mother was saying. She was already going to a favorite place in her mind's eye: the place she would miss the most. On one of their family excursions, they had seen chimpanzees in the rainforests of Nyungwe National Park. Abby loved the Kamiranzovu waterfall there—the way you could barely hear anything over the roar of the falling water. Her mother had said that it was the very beginning of the River Nile.

Abby's favorite place of all, though, was the trail where you could walk through the treetops. On one walk amid the leaves, she and her family had seen blue monkeys at close enough range to examine the details of their sad-looking little faces.

Another time when they had visited the rainforest, her father had pointed out a tiny owl. "Look, Abby," he had whispered, handing her the binoculars. "On that branch over there. It's an Albertine owlet. There are very few of them left in the world, and they are rarely seen. Never forget that this owl honored you, me, and your mother by showing itself to us. It's a very special thing." From that day on, the Albertine owlet had been Abby's favorite bird.

Now, upon hearing the news that they would be leaving Rwanda, Abby jumped up from the table, crying, "Please, Mommy, no!" and bolted out the door. She ran until she was out of breath and could go no further. Finding herself standing at the base of an ancient eucalyptus tree, Abby crumpled to the ground, sobbing. The medicinal scent of the crisp leaves came wafting up from where she had crushed them beneath her knees. A bird alighted nearby, and Abby recognized it as the variable sunbird by its bright yellow belly, purple breast, and jewel-like shining green head.

～

ABBY CONTINUED TO WANDER in a daze. Her heart felt as though it had been ripped open. She looked north and saw the towering peak of Mount Karisimbi, its nearly 15,000-foot crown hidden in the mist. She remembered how cold it had been the day she and her parents had hiked up the steep, rocky slope—how her world had changed when they saw the mountain gorillas and visited Dian Fossey's grave. Turning to her mother, the girl had asked, "Why did they kill her?"

Fiona knelt down, took Abby's hands in her own, and looked clearly into her eyes. "Because she fought so fiercely to protect the mountain gorillas. And she worked against the people who wanted to kill them."

"But why?"

"Dian Fossey loved the gorillas and the mountains where they live. She knew that without the gorillas, the soul of the mountains would vanish."

On that day, Abby found her heroine. She, too, loved these mountains and the wildlife that inhabited their misty slopes. A precocious reader from an early age, with her mother's help, Abby consumed every article and book she could find by or about Dian Fossey and her protection of the mountain gorillas. Her favorite passage from Fossey was the last thing she had written in her journal before she was killed: "When you realize the value of all life, you learn to dwell less on what is past and concentrate more on the preservation of the future."

The wild animals were Abby's friends. What would she do if she had to leave the only home she'd ever known? A voice inside her head screamed, *No! I won't go!* Deep down inside, though, Abby knew the truth: She loved her parents most of all, and would follow them wherever they needed to go so her mother could get well.

With this realization, Abby's anger dissolved into a powerful grief that wracked her small frame. She bent her head, auburn hair hanging like a shroud over her face. Tears poured down into the soil where her life had been nurtured—and from which it was about to be uprooted. Wiping them away, Abby looked up at the summit of Mount Karisimbi, whose veiled peak had always been a source of mystery. It inspired a longing in her for the sun to break through…a new day for her beloved mountain gorillas.

For now, the mist seemed to cast a dark cloud over what was to come: a future living in a foreign country where she would have to make a new home and learn to love a new land. Even as Abby's warrior self seethed with a fury that felt as though it could ignite the dry eucalyptus leaves, she could already sense the first uninvited glimmer of resignation. The Earth was beginning to shift beneath her. The life Abby had thought would always stay the same was about to become a part of her past. For the love of her mother and father, there was no way to resist what was happening or harbor any hope of remaining in Rwanda. Abby could feel part of her heart starting to tear away. Leaving the land she loved—her lifelong friends and beloved animals—felt for all the world as if she were leaving God.

1

Roger Lemieux's favorite pastime was bait-casting in the Cape Cod Canal at sunset. Apart from the rocky bluffs off of Beavertail in Jamestown, Rhode Island, he couldn't think of anywhere else he could drop a line into deep water so close to shore. There was something about watching the boats glide by and greeting folks on foot and bicycle as they passed.

Today, from his vantage point, it felt as if the world was moving around him as the rich-hued rays of late day cast a golden mantle across the surface of swiftly flowing tides. From that shore, awash in the scent of brine and seaweed, peace mingled with the anticipation of the next new experience that would come his way. All he had to do was watch and wait, rod in hand.

In the fading daylight at the end of this sultry drink of a late-summer evening, Roger greeted a jogger as she passed. His gaze lingered on the smooth cadence of long, lovely legs as his roving eye caught movement on the opposite shore, next to the Cape Cod Canal Power Plant. Roger's eyes lingered on a set of headlights bobbing along the access road that skirted the perimeter fence. After slowly weaving their way through the bumps and puddles left by a late-day rain shower, the headlights came to rest at the shore, where Roger knew there was clear access to the water.

It had always struck him as ironic that the fishing was so fine in the upwelling waters by the cooling towers. There must have been good eating for the fish where the warm outflow from the power plant met the cool salt water. His friends swore it was the best fishing location along the entire length of the canal, rhapsodizing about the size and number of fish they'd caught there.

Roger watched the headlights of the large light-colored SUV flicker out. In the waning light, he could just make out the dome light as the driver opened the door to disembark. Whoever it was wasn't wasting any time. Stepping quickly around to the rear and opening the hatch, the figure came back into view carrying a large bucket before walking to the water's edge and dumping something in. After the driver had made several more trips to offload whatever was in the back of the SUV, the dome light came back on, the head-lights glowed once again, and the driver gee-and-hawed a few times before heading back up the winding access road. As the lights finally lost themselves in a thicket of scrub oak and willow, Roger thought, *what could anyone possibly be dumping into the canal at this time of day?*

As he considered the possibilities, a tugboat labored past, leaving him shrouded in the lingering backwash of diesel fumes. If the figure had been carrying bags, Roger would have concluded that it was a load of trash someone had been trying to get rid of without having to pay the tipping fees, or a noxious substance that a local business was dumping illegally, figuring that no one would find it down at the end of a disused access road before it was carried away on the outgoing tide. No matter which idea he considered, however, nothing satisfied the nagging sense that something was not right.

A gull's raucous call broke his reverie, and Roger suddenly knew what he had to do. He reeled in his line, clipped one of the treble hooks onto an eyelet of the fishing rod, turned the reel handle, and flipped the bail wire to snug up the line before closing the bait box. Walking slowly back toward the parking access, he stowed his gear, started the engine, and drove toward the Sagamore Bridge.

~

IT WAS TWILIGHT NOW, and the late-evening traffic was light. From the height of the bridge's wide arc, Roger could see the last russets of day fading on the western horizon. There was a quality to the light on Cape Cod that he loved—a clarity he couldn't find closer to Boston.

Soon, his truck was rocking along the uneven access road by the power plant. At the dead end, Roger cut the engine and pulled a flashlight from his glove box. Opening the door, he stepped out onto a weedy path and walked toward the water's edge in the dim light of its beam. *Batteries are almost dead*, he surmised. Still, Roger could see the fresh imprint of what looked like someone's running shoes in the low muddy spots. At the end of the path, he crossed the bike trail and managed to find solid footing between the slimy, uneven rocks. As he aimed his flashlight beam into the water, the sight meeting his eyes rocked him back from the edge. He stumbled, muttering, "Holy shit."

After gathering himself, Roger finally found the courage to lean over and shine the light into the water once again. There, staring back at him, was a set of eyes. The pupils, prominent vertical slits, were framed by the features of a large feline he'd only ever seen at a zoo or in wildlife films. Roger found himself gazing into the eyes of an ocelot. Its cold, lifeless stare peered back from a severed head resting on a bed of entrails. Other body parts were strewn helter-skelter in the crevices of several large boulders.

The flashlight beam was now shaking in Roger's hand, and he could feel the stiff hairs on his neck standing alert. Sweat coated his palms as he turned and swept the beam across the path. Walking swiftly back to the truck, he stumbled in haste, his mind a terrified blur.

What if...whoever left this ungodly waste is still somewhere nearby, watching to see if anyone witnessed them dumping it? The thought threw Roger's mind over to a state of near-panic as his pickup jostled away from the nightmarish scene, tossing him about on the seat.

When his tires reached pavement, Roger gunned the engine and headed in the opposite direction from home just in case he was being followed. After a few miles, seeing no headlights in the rearview mirror, he slowed to the speed limit. When his heartbeat finally began to quell and he felt satisfied that no one was behind him, Roger turned the truck along a road that would take him home by a circuitous route.

A half-hour later, Roger angled up his driveway, comforted by the familiar sound of gravel crunching under tires. He flicked off the headlights, powered down the window, and listened: nothing but a great horned owl calling from the scrub, and the distant whine of a car amplified by the damp nocturnal air.

By daylight, the Cape was often bustling, busier than he liked; but after sunset, there were still a few places like Roger's home: remote, overgrown pockets ribboned with narrow back roads, lonely and even desolate in the misty, crepuscular air. When he pulled the door handle, the click resounded in the stillness, the noise rendered even more acute by the heightened state of his senses. Once inside his house, Roger turned the knob and listened as the deadbolt slid into place. It felt good to be home, and safe.

Even though the hour was late, he walked directly over to the cordless phone, picked it up, and sat down on the couch before dialing the number of the only person on the Cape who could help in a situation like this: Abigail Fiorelli. In all Roger's years on the force before he'd retired from police work, Abby, as she was known to her friends and close associates, was the best detective he'd ever encountered: sharp, undaunted, and, above all else, discreet to a fault. In the close communities on the Cape, the ability to keep a secret was paramount.

Roger heard Fiorelli pick up on the other end of the line,

her husky voice made richer by the languid tone of someone who had been disturbed from a deep sleep. "This had better be important," she said.

"Abby, I'm sorry to call at this hour, but I saw something tonight that scared the hell out of me, and you're the first person I could think of to call."

"What an honor," she replied. "Unless someone has murdered the pope, you'd better have a good reason." Roger heard Fiorelli yawn. After a long pause, she finally asked, "What is it?"

"I was fishing from my favorite spot along the canal. You know, across from the power station."

"Yes, what of it?" Fiorelli asked impatiently.

"You're not going to believe this," said Roger.

"Well, you're not going to believe what comes out of my mouth next unless you come to the point and let me get back to sleep."

2

The next morning, when Abigail Fiorelli opened her eyes, she flashed back to her late-night conversation with Roger Lemieux, wondering if it had been a dream or an incredibly annoying nightmare. She'd known Roger for a long time, and though she understood that he was sometimes bored in his retirement and missed the adrenaline rush of investigating a new crime, she also knew he wouldn't fabricate a story—nor would he call late at night unless it was extremely urgent.

Abby flipped back the bedcovers, swung her long legs over the edge of the bed, and headed for the bathroom. Brushing her teeth and looking in the mirror, she recognized in her own face the traits she'd inherited from her parents. Her auburn hair flowed richly down her shoulders and back—a luxurious mane that evoked her father's thick dark brown hair, burnished with russets from her mother's fiery locks. Her emerald green eyes were flecked with hazel, and her skin was a warm cream—a smooth blend of her mother's pale Scottish complexion and the olive hue her father had inherited from relatives still living in the rural hinterlands of southern Italy in the vicinity of Montecasino.

Abby had loved both of her parents deeply, each in her own way, but had always been drawn to the excitement of her father's police work and his godlike presence in the eyes of others as captain of the Barnstable police force. Sometimes, she thought the direction her life had taken had been pre-ordained by her name: Abigail, *joy of the father*, and Fiorelli, *little flower*.

Now, in her early thirties and a statuesque five feet ten inches, she'd had her share of lovers. Still, there was no shortage of suitors. Chris Armstrong was her latest, but he could only make the drive down from Boston on the occasional weekend. Some mornings, she missed opening her eyes to the early light, curled up in the comforting arms of someone to whom she felt attracted and about whom she cared deeply...someone she knew and trusted. Abby had yet to find a companion with that essential combination of qualities in just the right balance.

Abigail Fiorelli filled her time with other passions. She thrived on the hunt, searching for clues that would lead her down the path of putting away another thief, rapist, or murderer. Her keen eye for detail, for which she'd become famous as a detective, had been perfected by the observational skills she'd honed to a fine edge as an avid birder and student of nature.

A Harvard graduate who had majored in law and minored in forensic science, Abby took special interest in analyzing crime scenes by interpreting the signs recorded in nature: a torn leaf, a footprint in the shifting Cape sands, the scat or tracks of a particular animal. She was constantly amazed at how much other investigators missed because they were ignorant or uninformed about the natural world and its secrets just waiting to be discovered.

When she was ready to leave the house, Fiorelli climbed into her white Range Rover and drove toward The Blue Plate Diner on Barnstable's Main Street. The restaurant sat across the way from the complex of buildings that served as the county seat. As she turned into the parking lot, she slowed to let the elderly Mrs. Sims walk through the gap in the sidewalk where the driveway entered the parking lot. Mrs. Sims waved as she passed, tugging gently on the leash securing her Jack Russel terrier, Football. In the past, whenever Abby had asked Mrs. Sims how the dog had come to acquire such an unusual name, she would just say, "It's a long story, so I'll take a pass." Abby loved the subtle dry humor of the longstanding inhabitants of her hometown.

Abby entered the front door with her usual bearing. Some thought she had the grace of a dancer or model; others believed she was haughty. A few of the diners, seated in the long row facing the kitchen, turned and served up the usual flurry of stale morning salutations.

"Hey, Fiorelli."

"Did you forget your binoculars?"

"Who do you have in your sights this morning?"

As usual, Abby ignored everyone but good friends.

The Blue Plate was a classic eating establishment frequented by a cross-section of local color: carpenters and plumbers, administrative assistants, lawyers, even plaintiffs on break from the goings-on at the nearby probate and superior courts. The worn linoleum floor, complemented by 1970s-era wall paneling, had been painted over in an eggshell pastel accented by pale blue trim and a blue carpet. A high shelf arranged with blue plates stood over the space that served as a combination dining area and kitchen. Wobbly ceiling fans circulated the air above large stainless steel ovens and vent hoods.

"Abby, over here!"

Spotting Roger Lemieux in one of the booths, Fiorelli made her way across the room and slid into the seat across from her old friend and erstwhile partner in crime-solving.

"Mornin', Abby."

"This had better be worth a phone call in the middle of the night, Roger. And you know I usually spend some time birdwatching down at Sandy Neck before reporting to the station. Tell me what you saw."

By the time Roger had finished retelling the story about his experience along the shore by the Cape Cod Canal Power Plant, Abigail found herself subconsciously leaning forward and gripping the edges of the table, hard. "You're sure, Roger? An ocelot? Truly? This isn't one of your practical jokes?"

"I know how it sounds, Abby, but even I wouldn't wake you up in the middle of the night for a practical joke. Well, maybe...."

"Right," interrupted Fiorelli. "I believe you think you saw what you did last night."

"I don't *believe* I saw what I did last night. I *know* what I saw."

"Then are you going to pay for this breakfast you invited me to so we can head over to Sandwich and take a look at the scene in the light of day, before anyone happens by and destroys the evidence?"

"'Course. I got this."

Fiorelli looked at Roger and rolled her eyes. "I've got to run to the ladies' room. Be right back."

"Sounds good. I'll meet you at the car."

When Fiorelli had gone and Lemieux was polishing off his last bits of breakfast, he overheard a construction crew talking a few tables down. The conversation was about Abby.

"I wonder how many people she's put behind bars?" mused one.

"Why do you say that?" asked another.

"Because most men would kill just to spend one night in her company."

"I would, and then I'd be glad to do the time."

Lemieux opened his wallet, threw some money down on the table, and got up slowly from his seat. As he passed the cash register, he said to the waitress, "Thanks, Bev. The tab and tip are on the table."

"What's the rush, hon?" asked Bev.

"Believe me," Lemieux replied, "you don't want to know, and you wouldn't believe me if I told you."

"Oh, so it's like that," responded Bev with a send-off wink, her eyes gleefully flitting back and forth between

Lemieux and Fiorelli, who had emerged from the bathroom and was walking toward the front door.

Before going out to the car, Lemieux walked over to the other table, staring down at the men seated there. All conversation and motion stopped, forkfuls of food suspended halfway between plates and open mouths. One of the workers finally asked Lemieux, "Can we help you with something, buddy?"

"That's my partner you're talking about. She's one of the best detectives on the Cape. So how about showing some respect?" Without waiting for a response, Lemieux turned on his heel and stormed out of the restaurant.

3

As Fiorelli's white Range Rover made its way along Route 6A east, she and Lemieux rode quietly for a time. At length, Abby broke the silence. "And you would know an ocelot when you see one because?"

"Because I have a thing for cats, and I've read up on the different species."

"And?"

"They're beautiful, powerful animals. Cats are among the most feared predators on Earth. Tigers are one of the only creatures, along with polar bears, that still have human beings on their dinner menu. You probably understand."

"And how's that?" responded Fiorelli with a bemused expression that belied any impression of taking offense, which she was intentionally trying to convey.

"You seem like the kind of person who would like cats, is all I'm saying. Someone as...um...independent as you just seems like she would understand cats as opposed to, say, dogs."

Fiorelli couldn't stop the grin that was forcing its way out. "I don't know whether to slap you or take that as a compliment."

"Then it's a good thing we're almost there," Lemieux retorted. "I read online that the ocelot's habitat ranges from Mexico all the way down to South America. They've disappeared from many places they once lived, and there are only about a hundred left in the southwestern U.S." Lemieux paused for a time as if considering the fate of the ocelot, then added, "Take the next left down that dirt track, about a quarter mile after you pass the main gate of the power plant."

In the flat light of the late summer morning, the heat was rising, and everything looked as innocent as the goldfinches flushing up from wild thistles as the Range Rover passed. Fiorelli thought about how the day-glo yellow birds waited all summer long to begin nesting just as their favorite food, thistle seeds, became available. She'd always wondered how this fascinating behavior could have evolved in one particular songbird when most other species began nesting as soon as they were able in the springtime. Hearing a high-pitched gull-like cry overhead, she pointed upward and exclaimed, "Look, an osprey!"

"Also known as a fishhawk, right?" queried Lemieux.

"Roger, I'm impressed."

"Hey, you're not the only person who spends time outdoors. I know my way around these wild parts pretty well. Where do you think my mind goes when I'm spending all those hours fishing?" Fiorelli opened her mouth to say something, but Lemieux cut her off. "Not a word."

"Not about you, Roger. About the osprey. Did you know that when osprey and bald eagles were more common in

New England, before DDT wiped them out over most of their range, eagles often perched nearby as ospreys caught their fish? The eagle would swoop in and steal fish from the osprey. Both species have made a comeback, and I now see that pilfering behavior pretty often."

"No, I didn't know that, but it goes to show."

"How's that?" asked Fiorelli.

"The bald eagle is a symbol of our government, right?"

"And?"

"We do all the work, then Uncle Sam swoops in and takes away most of the spoils," quipped Lemieux. "There, take that next left down the dirt track."

The Range Rover swayed and rolled as the pair traversed the unpaved access road with its numerous potholes and puddles. When they reached the shore of the Cape Cod Canal, Lemieux got out first, coming around to catch Fiorelli before she had the chance to walk over to the water's edge.

"Abby, listen to me. I'll show you where to look, but brace yourself."

"Okay," she responded. "We both need to watch where we step. I want to take some imprints."

Lemieux walked carefully down a barely-visible trail and peered over the edge into the water around the angular rocks. He stared for a time, took a long, deep breath, and motioned for Fiorelli to come stand next to him. She slowly arched her neck forward and gasped, holding her hand over her mouth to stifle a groan.

After a long pause during which neither of them spoke,

Fiorelli exclaimed, "Oh, my God, Roger. No matter how many crime scenes I investigate, it always hits me hard when I see something that shows me there's a new level of hell that people will stoop to." Then, gathering herself, she added, "I'm going to get my evidence kit."

When Fiorelli returned from the Range Rover, Lemieux watched with curiosity as she placed a large cooler on the ground, well away from the crime scene. Always prepared, Fiorelli kept the cooler in the rear hatch of her SUV just in case she needed it for forensic fieldwork. Opening the lid, she reached in, slipped on a pair of latex gloves, and pulled out several large clear self-sealing plastic bags. She handed a pair of latex gloves to Lemieux, saying, "Here. Put these on."

As Lemieux donned the gloves, he asked, "What do you want me to do?"

Fiorelli gave him several of the plastic bags and a black permanent marker.

"Go over to the remains and write down a visual categorization of everything you see: head, entrails, and so on. Use your cell phone to photo-document and GPS all the evidence in place. Shoot from several angles. Get closeups and some overview shots. Once you're done documenting everything where it lies, label each individual bag according to body part, then place each of them into the corresponding bag."

"And what are you going to do?"

"I'm going to photo-document the tire tracks and shoe-prints. Then I'll mix up some medium and take a few casts."

As Lemieux began the grisly task, the sight and meaty

smell of what he was handling nearly caused him to retch, but he steeled his nerves and reminded himself to stay on task.

Nearby, Fiorelli pulled out some water, a pail, a container of dry powder, and a wooden stirring spoon. She mixed up a batch of casting medium and went over to the most intact tire track she could find, pouring in the viscous material while making sure to obtain the proper thickness and coverage. It made her feel a little queasy when she considered that one of the most common uses for this type of material was the preservation of dental impressions.

Fiorelli repeated the same procedure with the most distinct sneaker track she could find: one that marked clearly where the creep had walked while carrying out this horrific deed. While the casts were setting, she continued photographing the crime scene. After waiting about fifteen minutes, she tested the casting material that had been poured into the tire track, found that it was firm, and carefully lifted it up, preserving a precise impression of what had been recorded in the surface of the soil.

As Fiorelli was lifting up the sneaker-track mold, she noticed a fresh cigarette butt that had been put out by a heel—crushed within a sneaker track next to the one from which she'd just gathered the impression, a few feet beyond the furthest reach of the tire tracks in the damp soil.

Looking closely, she saw that the filter was wrapped in gold paper. An insignia bearing the initials *NS* ringed its base. The first two letters of a word, *SH*, started down the shaft of the cigarette, proceeding below the filter to the burn line. The paper itself was a distinctive yellow. Fiorelli recognized the exclusive brand and picked it up with a pair of tweezers from her evidence pouch so she could bag the butt, too. As the acrid scent reached her nostrils, she marveled at how something as pleasingly and sweetly aromatic as cured tobacco could smell so wretched after it had burned. Fiorelli held the evidence bag up for Lemieux to see. "Roger, come take a look at this."

Lemieux walked over and stared at the butt for a long moment. His eyes drifted up to meet Fiorelli's. She knew that quizzical look; he didn't have to say a word. Abby waited as the tension lines between his eyes deepened. "Well?" he asked.

"The initials in the logo at the top of the colored paper, *NS*, and the first two letters just below the logo, *SH*, mean we're dealing with an exclusive brand called Nat Sherman. The rest of the letters in *Sherman's* were burned off when the cigarette was smoked."

"What about the yellow paper?" he inquired.

"Nat Sherman makes an especially high-end cigarette called Fantasia. Whoever is smoking these paid an exorbitant price."

"So you think he's well off?" asked Lemieux.

"She."

"Why she?"

"Fantasia cigarettes come in several different colors. They're marketed exclusively to women," replied Fiorelli.

"So we're dealing with a cigarette brand that's the Mazda Miata of smokes?"

"Exactly. There are chick cars…and chick butts."

"Now you're talking, Fiorelli."

"Don't go through that door, Roger, please."

"But you opened the door, not me."

"My mistake. The first thing that you stick through that kind of open door is always your…well…let's just say it's not your intellect. And I'll slam the door hard on your you-know-what if you don't let it rest."

By the time Fiorelli was done gathering evidence, Lemieux had completed his work and loaded the plastic bags into the cooler.

"We can search this tread track in our database to see what kind of tire created it, and cross-match it with the SUVs that tend to run that tire," he said.

"We can do the same with the footprint to trace the brand and style of shoe our suspect was wearing. Then…." Fiorelli stopped short as her eye caught something glistening in the early morning sunlight. She bent down to pick it up, holding it in her gloved hand and showing it to Lemieux. "It looks like a necklace pendant," she remarked.

"But what does it mean?"

"I don't know, offhand," replied Fiorelli. "But it looks like some kind of iconographic symbol—a dagger bookended by two outward-facing crescent moons."

"It's pretty distinctive," said Lemieux. "We should be able to research its origins and the meaning behind it."

"You're right. Meanwhile, we can't waste any time with these remains in my Rover. I'm going to stop at the bait shop down by Pairpoint Glassworks and pick up a bag of ice to pour into the cooler."

Having worked with Fiorelli on a number of cases, Lemieux knew that the wheels of her mind would already be turning. He admired the keenly analytical way she interpreted evidence—and her ability to make connections no one else saw. She had an encyclopedic memory filled with esoterica and details she'd memorized about things few others would even have thought helpful.

"Don't get me wrong when I say this, Abby. I only speak from the experience of working with you, but you handle this kind of thing with a pretty cool head, once you dive in."

Fiorelli stared directly into Lemieux's dark brown eyes. "It's my job."

After moving along the road in silence for a piece, Lemieux could feel the tension building between them. "Wellll…" he began.

"Well, what?" responded Fiorelli.

"Don't make me ask twenty questions, Fiorelli. You know what I'm asking. What is your early take on who this gal might be?"

"Gal, Roger? What gal? I'm assuming you meant to say *woman*."

"Like I said, we need to determine which make and model of car tends to come with that particular tire, but that could be tricky. Unless it's a fairly new car, the tires could have been swapped out for a different brand when they became worn out or were replaced."

"This owner could probably afford to replace the old tires with new ones of the same brand," said Fiorelli, "but I don't think that will even be a factor here."

"How so?"

"Because this individual could probably afford to replace the car before the first set of tires wore out."

"And how the hell did you make that determination?" exclaimed Lemieux. "Excuse my French."

"Simple," answered Fiorelli. "Did I mention just how much Fantasia cigarettes actually cost?"

"Not exactly." After a long pause, Lemieux implored, "WELL?"

"Upwards of forty dollars a pack, so we're dealing with a very wealthy individual."

"How did you come to know that brand?"

"One thing I noticed early on in my investigations, when providing evidence and testimony for the DA, is that people who commit crimes tend to engage in high-risk behaviors in other aspects of their lives."

"Such as?"

"Such as smoking. So I studied the characteristics of the various brands, especially those that would appeal to individuals with expensive taste."

"Because this kind of suspect would have the means to afford those kinds of smokes?" asked Lemieux.

"Right. And also because they tend to like to use their ill-begotten spoils to buy clothes, cars, and accessories that make an individual statement."

Lemieux instinctively sat up straight, folding his hands across his lap. After a long pause, he asked soberly, "How could anyone do something like this, and why would they do it?"

"At this point, I don't know," said Fiorelli. "But I'll promise you one thing. We're going to run this one down."

Lemieux saw the fire in Fiorelli's eyes. "Not to mention," he said, "that whoever is involved in this twisted business ruined a perfectly good night of fishing for me. I don't think that fishing spot will ever be the same."

4

Fiorelli swung by the Barnstable Police Station to drop off the evidence and catch up on the backlog of work from her other cases. The station was situated a few miles out of town, far from the cluster of local and federal buildings at the county seat of the historic town center. Whenever she had to testify at a major trial in superior court, Fiorelli couldn't help but feel moved as she walked up the granite steps to the grand portico framing the entrance. It was supported by four massive fluted columns that achieved the intended effect of elevating the eyes skyward, as if to reflect the moral high ground of the law.

The police station itself was a typical modern municipal building that rose two stories and stretched some 200 feet. As she approached the door, Fiorelli looked up to the glass-walled vestibule, reading the round bronze seal bearing a date that always impressed her. *Seal of the Town of Barnstable, Mass., 1639.* It was amazing to think that Barnstable had been founded less than twenty years after the Pilgrims set foot on the soil of the New World. *A fresh start for the Pilgrims,* she thought, *but not so great for the Wampanoag.*

Entering the double glass doors into the spacious foyer,

Fiorelli smiled as her gaze fixed upon the glimmering three-tiered brass chandelier. Had the architect been trying to make suspects feel as if they were arriving at a nice hotel?

"Hi, Rhonda. How's it going?" Abby greeted the receptionist seated behind one of three bulletproof glass screens. The central panel featured a mousehole cut into the bottom edge. Through it, one could push keys, wallets, and other belongings.

"Hey, Abby. I cahn't complain. Just anotha mawnin' sittin' behind this glass hav'n a wicked awesome time. How's about you?"

"Got one of those cases that makes my skin crawl. Other than that, peachy keen."

Fiorelli signed in at the window, sidestepping toward the staff door on the left that led to the suite of offices beyond. On the way inside, she found herself smiling, as she often did after talking to Rhonda. Even though she'd spent most of her life on the Cape, Abby had also lived in different parts of the world—wherever her parents' missionary work called for them to be stationed. She didn't have much of a regional accent, and even sounded to many locals like the folks Cape Codders referred to as *newcomahs*. Rhonda, however, had one of the best mid-Cape accents of anyone Fiorelli knew who had grown up there. She was an *oldcomah*.

When she saw the *Ladies* sign on a door, Fiorelli realized that she'd been out all morning without stopping into a bathroom. After finding some relief, she walked over to the sink, turned on the cold water faucet, and splashed her face.

It felt good—clean and refreshing. As she was drying off, she caught her expression in the mirror and realized how tired she appeared. *This job is going to make an old woman out of me.*

After coming out of the ladies' room, Fiorelli turned left, entering the corridor leading to the forensics lab. Inside, Andrew Coleman was peering into a dissecting microscope at some fibers from another case. He looked up when Fiorelli stepped in.

"Hey, Abby. What've you got for me today? Something interesting, I hope?"

"What are you working on?"

"IDing these fibers for a court case. All they have right now are circumstantials, so a lot rides on whether these match the fibers on the suspect's clothing. What have you got there?"

Fiorelli handed Coleman the plastic bags containing the cigarette butt and pendant. Then she passed him a larger bag containing the imprint of the shoe. "See if you can pull any fingerprints off this butt, or from the pendant. And let me know what you find for the make of the shoe that made these tracks. Once you've checked the butt for prints, test to see if there's enough DNA present on the filter to run a profile. Roger is working on matching the tire track to the makes and models of vehicles that run that specific tire."

"Anything else?"

"Yes, but I've got it on ice, pending a necropsy."

Andrew pushed his chair back from the lab table and looked directly at Fiorelli. "Is this a murder?"

"Yes, but not what you're thinking."

"Then what?"

"The remains of a butchered ocelot."

Coleman stood up and walked over to Fiorelli. "No kidding! Let me see."

"Only if you promise not to say a word to anyone. I don't want to start a game of telephone with the media as a receiver on the other end of a sordid chain."

Out in the parking lot, Andrew peered down into the back of the Range Rover as Fiorelli pulled the lid off the cooler. He paled. Abby could tell he'd stopped breathing. Andrew took a few quick steps away from the car, turned away from Fiorelli, and vomited.

Once Coleman had stopped wretching, Abby handed him a few tissues from the box she kept in her car. Turning toward her, he said, "Oh, man, that is really sick. And I thought I'd seen just about everything on this job. Where'd you find this?"

"It's premature to discuss the details, but I've got to get this over to the medical examiner's office ASAP."

"Why don't you let me drop it off? It will give me a good excuse to get out of the office."

"Thanks, Andrew. I'll owe you big on this one. Make sure they sign off on the confidentiality waiver. This can't get out yet. Got it?"

Coleman nodded.

Fiorelli walked out the door and headed for the office of Chief Martin Morales. She was going to need a partner on this investigation, and it was only fair that Lemieux also be assigned to the case. Though Lemieux was officially retired, he was frequently hired as a consultant to work on cases that overlapped with his base of knowledge and years of experience as an investigator. Fiorelli had worked with Lemieux on several cases. She was always impressed by the insight he had gained over the course of his long career and the breadth of information he had absorbed in divergent fields related to criminal behavior. When she arrived at Chief Morales' office, Abby knocked firmly, but not too loudly, on the door.

"Come." Morales' response rang out in his familiar baritone. Fiorelli thought her boss's voice reflected his management style perfectly: authoritative and strong, yet personable and considerate. As she entered, Morales gestured to a chair in front of his desk. Without looking up from his work, he said, "Have a seat."

At length, Morales put down his pen and looked at Fiorelli. "How are you?"

"I'm fine, Chief. And you?"

"I'm good. Now, what can I do for you?" Fiorelli ran through the events that had occurred to date in the ocelot case. Morales listened intently, steepling his fingers in front of his lips. When she had finished, Morales paused a minute or two, contemplating the pictures and events Fiorelli had conjured in his mind's eye. "I don't know if these offbeat situations find you, Fiorelli, or if you go looking for them, but you definitely come to me with some fascinating cases. How can I help?"

"I realize Inspector Lemieux is retired, but he does consult from time to time on cases for which he possesses expertise. I could use his help on this case."

"And you don't think any of the other investigators could come in?"

"Perhaps," Abby replied, making sure not to dismiss her superior's suggestion out of hand. "However, Roger has the background for this case, and early indications show that this investigation is going to demand complete attention and consume a considerable amount of time."

"You do realize that the district has been tightening the screws on our budget?"

"Yes, and I wouldn't ask if I didn't think it was important."

Fiorelli watched as Morales pondered the situation. She could almost see his thoughts leaning toward the affirmative. Before he had been promoted to the position of chief, Morales had worked side by side with Lemieux on many cases over the years. Morales had great respect for his former partner's work and always looked forward to an opportunity to collaborate, even if their relationship on this particular case would be tangential.

"Approved. But don't let me see any three-martini lunches show up in the expense logs." Morales offered a wry smile, knowing that Fiorelli was frugal and didn't even drink much in her personal life.

"Thank you, Chief."

"Anything else?"

"I just want to say how much I appreciate...."

Before she could finish, Morales had picked up his pen, raised both hands in mock surrender, and dismissed Fiorelli with a friendly wave.

～

BACK IN HER OFFICE, Fiorelli forced the images of the ocelot out of her mind, bearing down on the mountain of paperwork and screen time that had been accumulating. She truly hated mundane case-related paperwork and requisition forms, but knew things only got worse when she put them off.

After she'd been at it long enough to feel that she'd made some decent headway, Fiorelli went online to research images that combined the crescent moon with the tip of a dagger. First, she tried searching for daggers and moons, but came up with pages of advertisements for hunting knives and cultish ritual moon daggers. Then she tried adding ocelots into the mix. Nothing. Finally, she took a different tack, and began looking up symbols for hunting and the moon. After viewing a number of web pages that described the impact of the lunar cycle on deer hunting—and some links that forced her to backtrack away from tawdry softcore porn sites prompted by the keywords *hunting* and *moon*—Abby realized that the morning was flying by. She opened a container of yogurt and ate it slowly until the online research began to lead her in circles.

Frustrated and feeling the need to clear her head, Fiorelli left the station, walked south on Phinney's Lane, and turned into a maze of roads and cul-de-sacs that wound through a suburban neighborhood composed of large, expensive houses. A mockingbird was singing from an electric wire, and Fiorelli tried to identify each of the birdcalls mimicked in its rapid-fire song: phoebe, chickadee, cardinal, red-tailed hawk, and so on. Appreciating the quiet as she walked along the tree-lined streets, Abby often wondered what really went on inside these households that appeared so peaceful and civil to the outside observer. Then she checked those thoughts, reminding herself that they were a pitfall in her line of work.

Back at the station, Fiorelli resumed chipping away at the mind-numbing deskwork. The only way she could tolerate it was to think of it as a process rather than an end point. Abby reminded herself that no matter how much one loved one's work, every job had its unpleasant attributes. Still, she was relieved when it was time to head home.

5

Home, to Fiorelli, was a modest shingle-sided house that had started its existence as a three-season vacation cottage. It sat along the edge of a barrier pond behind expansive dunes stretching for several miles. The location was separated from Cape Cod Bay by the dunes and Sandy Neck Beach, a popular destination for swimming and the only place Abby knew of on the entire Cape where people could still drive down to a beach and go camping.

In the late 1900s, most of the original seasonal cottages had been sold off, but Fiorelli had inherited her family's cottage. She loved it just the way it was: rustic, cozy, and perched on a high rise behind the dunes, closer to the ocean than any of the McMansions that had sprung up around it. Even the old, decrepit remains of cement and cable guardrails that lined Sandy Neck Road access appealed to her sense of days gone by. A few posts were missing so much concrete that only naked vertical pieces of rebar still protruded from the ground.

Fiorelli didn't want to miss the late-day birding along the hiking trail that wound behind and through the dunes. She grazed a quick snack from the fridge, grabbed her binoculars, and sauntered out along the margins of a nearby marsh.

As she made her way along the trail, Abby passed an interpretive sign indicating that back in 1640, recently-arrived Europeans had "bought" Sandy Neck from the Wampanoag for *3 axes & 6 coats*. Fiorelli knew that the Natives had only traded the *right* to use the land for hunting, fishing, and gathering, and that colonists had illicitly used English law to lay claim to every plot of land they could get their hands on. The thought of this historic deceit still made her angry. She had also read that Roger Williams hadn't been kicked out of Massachusetts just for his religious beliefs. He had also been an outspoken critic of the way land was being stolen from Native peoples for a song, when in fact, only the rights to use that land had been purchased.

Along the trail, Fiorelli heard and saw many of the familiar birds that dwelt in the complex of habitats by the shore, where pitch pine, red cedar, and scrub oak gave way to bayberry and salt spray rose. A catbird mewed its uncannily feline cry as a kingbird swooped down from a tree and snapped up a damselfly. Chipping sparrows were flitting about in a low brushy area at the edge of a carpet of beach heather adjacent to a low sandy opening where Abby had followed the progress of a nesting pair of horned larks earlier that summer. A cardinal's loud whistle arose from a dense stand of beach plum.

Once she reached the shore of the marsh and found herself standing at the margin of the dunegrass and salt marsh hay, the turnings of Abby's mind wound down. She became lost in the sound of the wind, the briny smell of cord grass, and the occasional cry of a gull. There was something freeing about being out in the wild, engaged in one of the only pleasurable pursuits she had in her life. Birding released Abby's mind from any particular thing or person, and liberated something creative inside her in the midst of a timeless place.

As she watched a snowy egret wading in the shallows where slender reeds and azure sky reflected in the water, Abby thought, *how could anyone have ever killed these amazing birds just for the thrill of the hunt, or to tuck a few of their plumes into a hatband?* Even John James Audubon, she had read, had shot as many as fifty or more birds of each species he'd painted, just to obtain representative samples of the differences in appearance between individuals. *Thank God, times have changed.*

Scanning the edge of the water through her binoculars, Abby enjoyed the mirrored reflection of the slender marsh rushes along the pond's surface and the swooping shapes of tree swallows dipping down to feed upon insects. *An artist couldn't possibly have painted a more beautiful picture.* The word *artist* stuck in her mind and wouldn't let go. What connection could possibly exist between hunters and artists? Different ways of relating to nature, of making a connection to the wild? *No, that's too far-fetched. Artists appreciate nature and leave it as they find it, but hunters have to destroy something in order to enjoy it.*

Then, in a singular moment of awareness, information Abby had gleaned from her research finally coalesced, and the connection came to her in perfect clarity: Artemis.

The pendant they had found at the crime scene depicting a pair of moons on either side of a dagger...wasn't really a dagger at all. It was the tip of an arrow, the classic symbol of Artemis, Greek goddess of the hunt. Artemis was also the moon goddess, and had been Fiorelli's favorite figure in Greek mythology ever since she'd first learned about her in the fifth grade. On more than one occasion, Fiorelli had fantasized about using Artemis's bow and arrow on some of the obnoxious boys who had pursued her relentlessly around the schoolyard during recess.

What could Artemis possibly have to do with this particular case? That may be the tip of an arrow, but I also have a feeling it's just the tip of the iceberg.

As Abby walked up the narrow trail leading from the dunes back to her cottage, she realized that it was Friday, and Chris would soon be arriving for the weekend. Chris Armstrong, her significant other, was an ecologist who taught biology at Harvard.

Even though Fiorelli had also attended Harvard, she had first met Chris while taking classes at the University of Michigan Law School. Though Chris had been a post-doctoral student in the biology department studying the migratory habits of Kirtland's warbler and several other bird species impacted by climate change, the law school had recruited him. In forensics class, he had shown an uncanny aptitude for solving cases by reading evidence from the natural world, including plant species, animal signs, soil types, seeds, microbes, and other biological and physical clues from the wild.

This connection to nature was something elemental Abby and Chris shared, but their relationship went deeper than that. She had encountered Chris during a time when he was instructing a practicum he'd developed to complement a legal class on physical evidence—finding and analyzing clues in the natural world.

Abby had immediately been attracted to him, and enjoyed being able to watch him for long periods of time as her instructor. At one point, in a lab involving latex molds of animal tracks, Chris had come over to answer one of her questions. At six foot two, he leaned in over her to examine her work. Feeling his presence that close, smelling the outdoors on his clothes combined with his pleasant, faintly musky scent, Abby felt a wave of heat rise inside of her. It forced a blush she'd hoped he wouldn't notice.

Earlier this morning, Abby had called Chris to discuss the case of the ocelot. "Hi, it's me, Abby."

"Oh, really?" he responded. "As opposed to all the other women who call me, whose voices sound exactly like the one person I've been dying to see?"

After a brief pause, Abby replied, "Do all of your compliments have to be so convoluted?"

"Why? Things got pretty convoluted between us last weekend when I was visiting, and you didn't seem to mind."

"Okay, enough," said Fiorelli. "I'd like your help solving

a case that has me puzzled. There's a fair amount of evidence, but nothing has begun to connect yet."

"What is the crime?"

"Honestly, it's one of the most disturbing scenes I've ever encountered, and you know we've seen some pretty gruesome field cases."

"Don't remind me. Would you rather discuss it in person?"

"That all depends on what you mean by *discuss*."

"I think you know exactly what I mean."

"Chris, this case is different. I'm afraid the evidence is pointing to something bigger than just an isolated instance."

"Are you free this weekend?"

"Available, but not free. Would you like to come over to my place?"

"When?"

"How about sixish?"

"I'll see you then. And Abby…I know you don't like to ask for help, and I'm glad you felt free to call. But try not to let this case get to you, whatever it is."

"I'm working on it."

"Bye, Abby."

"Bye, Chris."

After she hung up the phone, Fiorelli realized that the conversation had prompted thoughts of her father and his propensity for philosophizing and relating his work to his faith. She could almost hear his thoughts on the case. *There is something deeper here. But of darkness, not of light.*

Abigail's father, Angelo, an Episcopalian minister,

had always quoted the Bible from memory. Most evenings during her childhood, he had chosen a topic for the family to discuss. As Abby grew older, discussion often blossomed into debate. Challenged by her father's quick mind, she had learned everything possible about his faith, studying the Bible until she could quote it chapter and verse. Later, she'd explored other religions in order to use different types of wisdom to embellish and inform her arguments.

Her mother had died of cancer when Abby was only eleven, and she still struggled whenever she thought of her. Now, in the best of times, the world just stopped; at the worst, her eyes would tear up. She sometimes found herself weeping over the ache inside, or smiling at a long-cherished memory of a shared moment: strolling along the beach or working in her mother's lush garden. The hole in Abby's heart left by the loss of her mother was still fully present. She'd spent more than twenty years building a life around that void while guarding her memories as fiercely as she had loved her mother in life.

6

Abby was relieved to hear a knock at the door. When she looked out the window, she saw Chris standing there and waving. She felt her heart quicken as she turned the knob to let him in.

"Hi, sweetie," he said, eyes alight.

"You look like you're in a good mood," Abby observed.

"It's been a long week, but I'm finally in the arms of the one person I've been dying to see since I left last Sunday."

"Well, here I am." Chris reached down and kissed her deeply. Abby pulled back.

"What is it?" he asked.

"This case I'm working on is really upsetting."

Chris took Abby's hand and led her over to the couch. When they were both seated, he leaned in, suggesting, "Perhaps there's something I could do to help take your mind off the case."

"Perhaps."

"Ye of little faith."

"Oh, I have plenty of faith. It's just a matter of where I place it."

Chris came close and kissed her languorously. Abby

felt something give inside of her. As they lay back, their hands drifted off to find familiar places as the rest of the world slipped away. Slowly and deliberately, as he always did while continuing to kiss her, Chris undressed Abby, and she reciprocated. His mouth left hers and worked its magic on all the high points of her topography, causing her to moan.

"Am I hurting you?" Chris asked playfully. "Because I could stop."

"No—quite the opposite. Keep going."

Abby loved looking into his warm brown eyes and running her hands through his thick, sandy curls. There was something about the way he took his time, gradually pulling her under his spell, the anticipation and excitement building until she felt a tremendous desire for release. His tongue moved into the darkest recesses of her center, and then he was inside.

As a biologist, Abby understood the ways in which nerves and synapses interface with skin, hormones, and scent to create the element of pleasure we know as making love, but she had always marveled at the fact that there was no accounting for the sheer intensity and sublime feeling of the act itself. As she felt herself approaching climax, she pictured her most intimate core as finely woven threads of silver and chocolate. When she peaked, her sensations exploded outward to a place that was sweet, light, and electric. Afterward, as she lay with Chris still inside her, she asked, "What are you thinking?"

"Mostly, I'm just feeling full and close to you."

"But you seem like you've drifted off."

"Well, I am daydreaming a little."

"About what?"

"About how one day, I'm going to travel the world as a forensic biologist, solving the mysteries of nature in far-away places."

"And...?"

"And..." said Chris with a mischievous smile, "meet lots of exotic women."

Abby slapped him playfully on the shoulder. "Not on my watch!"

"Not to worry. It would all be in the interest of biological research, related to my studies of the mating habits of various avian species."

"And what's wrong with the fieldwork you're conducting right now? Isn't this good enough for your research?"

"Perhaps, but I believe further investigation is required. It's a rather nascent hypothesis, and I'm anxious to see if it can be scientifically proven that making love requires heat."

"How so?"

"Well, you know I've studied the mating habits of the Kirtland warbler."

"Of course."

"And how they nest in jack pine habitat...."

"What of it?"

"Those trees can only drop their seeds if their cones are opened by fire."

Their eyes caught. Abby smiled and placed the palm of

her hand on the round of his chest. She liked that his body felt lithe from running, not bulked up like a weightlifter. She pulled Chris toward her and kissed him again with surprising intensity, indulging his newfound passion for mutual biological research. His movements while making love mirrored the way he moved about in the world: with a fluid grace Abby found extremely sensuous. At times like this, his relaxed, laid-back self intensified into a smoldering passion that complemented her own.

Abby surprised herself by saying, "I think your eyes are my favorite part of you."

"Why's that?"

"When our eyes connect—when we're, you know, in the moment—I feel like you open up and I can really see you."

"And what about the rest of me?"

"Well, I guess it will just have to suffice."

CHRIS AND ABBY'S TIME together always ended too soon. Fiorelli now found herself staring at the receding taillights of the vintage 1960 Corvette convertible Chris drove when he wasn't out doing fieldwork. The two of them loved tooling around the narrow winding roads on the Cape, the hills of Western Massachusetts, or wherever their occasional trips brought them. The curvaceous baby blue lines of the car slipped through the air as smoothly as bird's wings.

Corvettes today are interesting cars, but they have nothing over the early models, Abby thought. She had heard others say the car was a classic, and that the brand was never the same after they started making the bodies out of fiberglass, but she knew that wasn't what had killed the Corvette. It had happened when the design turned away from gorgeous curves in favor of sharp edges. Abby consistently gravitated toward things that reminded her of the simple economy and elegance of the shapes she saw in nature. Her favorite buildings had been created by Gaudi, the iconic Spanish architect. Few people knew that the spirals, hexagons, and other shapes and patterns that inspired his designs were based upon the numbers of the Fibonacci Sequence.

Edges. I don't like edges. While Abby loved her time with Chris, their all-too-brief encounters usually seemed to end with her standing at the edge of alone, wondering where their relationship was heading. Later that day, Abby found herself looking up at a leaden late-summer sky, which, she realized, reflected her mood perfectly. The hoarse call of a green heron rose up from the shore of a distant marsh. A light breeze was blowing in from the dunes, redolent of salt and seaweed. The scent was pungent and somewhat rank, but it reminded Abby that she was home.

Back inside, Fiorelli sat down to one of her favorite weekly indulgences: small spoonfuls of rich coffee ice cream while reading the *Boston Sunday Globe*. If you took the time, it was amazing what you could find in the newspaper. For her, it was the printed version of strolling along the high-tide line and combing through tons of flotsam and jetsam for the unique treasure that made it all worthwhile.

7

No matter how she tried, Abby couldn't concentrate. Thoughts of Chris were roiling her mind, together with a longing for the kind of companionship she had only found with her few close friends. On impulse, she decided to call Rhonda.

Even though they were different in so many ways, the two women shared a connection. Rhonda was like the sister Abby had never had. While Abby was a driven graduate of Harvard Law, Rhonda had attended a two-year program to become certified as a law enforcement dispatcher. Abby loved children, but was becoming concerned about her biological clock. Rhonda had gotten married in her early twenties and had three wonderful kids: two girls and a boy, all of whom loved Abby like a favorite aunt.

Abby knew that some people thought she had a brilliant legal mind, but Rhonda possessed innate native intelligence and insight about people that Abby admired. Abby had been born while her parents were serving as missionaries in Rwanda, and developed her expansive worldview because of the traveling they'd done together as a family. Rhonda had lived in Barnstable her entire life; she knew everyone and everything there was to know about life mid-Cape.

Abby picked up the phone and dialed Rhonda's number. After just two rings, she heard her friend's familiar voice.

"This had bettah be good, Abby," said Rhonda in a nasal tone accentuated by the tinny sound of the receiver.

"I forgot you had caller ID," said Abby.

"Of cawse I do. I spend all day at the station havin' tah ansah calls from every reprobate who lives around he-ah, but you know I don't pick up at home unless it's someone I wanna talk to."

"I don't blame you."

"So, how ah you doin', Abby? Let's see, it's Sunday evening, so that means Chris has probably just headed back up to Bahston. Am I right?"

"I hate the way you can see right through me."

"The kids are all either watchin' TV or in the middle of a trance on some electronic device or anothah. Do you want to come ovah and tawk?"

"I'd love to."

"See yah in a bit." Rhonda rang off.

Abby drove across town beneath a spectacular lingering sunset. As she crossed the bridge over Scorton Creek, she saw a great blue heron rising up from the riparian reeds. It flew low and steady across the space in front of her car, its pterodactyl-like silhouette haloed in the fading light.

Great blues were one of two species that allowed Fiorelli to be easily convinced when paleontologists and ornithologists had determined that birds evolved from dinosaurs. This view had been reinforced when she'd read about fossils discovered in China that clearly showed nascent dinosaur wings with feathers. And for their part, wild turkeys reminded Abby of miniature velociraptors, the kind that hunted in packs and developed a taste for tourists in *Jurassic Park*.

As her thought sequence came full circle, Fiorelli recalled seeing the fossilized tracks of turkey-sized carnivorous dinosaurs still visible in the bedrock of Holyoke, Massachusetts—tracks made by roaming packs that had walked on two feet nearly 200 million years ago. She considered how insignificant life really was in relationship to the scale of geologic time.

～

RHONDA OPENED THE DOOR and ushered her friend into the living room. "Hey, Abby, come on in. Would you like a glass of wine? I've got this nice rosé someone gave me at last yeah's Christmas pahty. How's that sound?"

"That would be perfect."

Once they had settled in and taken a few sips, Rhonda broke the silence. "Things okay with you and Chris?"

"Yes, they're fine. We had a really nice weekend."

"So, why the long face?"

"I love him to death, but I'm just not sure where we're headed. I'm getting tired of watching those taillights driving away at the end of every visit."

"It'll happen. You guys ah pehfect togethah."

"I think so, too. Chris is the only man I've ever met who

really understands me. In fact, he's one of the only *people* who does. Him, and you."

"Thanks, sweetie. Listen, we had a pahty today for Piper's seventh behthday, and I picked up one of those chocolate mousse cakes they make special down at The Blue Plate. Would you like a piece?"

"God, yes."

Once the cake arrived, they each took a bite, moaning in delight.

"This is wicked good…almost as good as sex," Rhonda pronounced.

Fork paused mid-bite, Abby looked over at her friend. When their eyes met, they both burst out laughing. Abby laughed so hard she had to wipe tears from her eyes. "How do you do it?" she asked.

"You mean sex?"

"No, silly. I mean balancing everything: the kids, your job, time with Mark."

"I guess it comes natural from growin' up in a big family." Rhonda put her wine glass down and turned to face Abby. "So, what's this all about?"

"What—I can't just want to spend time with my best friend?"

"Honey, it's me, remembah?"

"I don't know, exactly. There's this empty feeling that comes up, like I said. It happened tonight when Chris drove away. Maybe it's because my mom has been gone for so many years, and it was just my father and my aunts raising me. I spent a lot of time on my own growing up, out on the beach and watching birds in the marshes. I still like time alone, and I don't really have a lot of friends outside of you. And I tend to be more comfortable around men than I am around women."

Rhonda finished the last bite of her cake and put down her fork. "Everybody's gawt hah own hist'ry. But when it comes down to it, we all need the same things—somethin' that makes us want to get out of bed in the mawnin', and people to love. Sometimes yaw too hahd on yawself. Time alone is good, and I know you love bein' out in naytchah and all, but maybe it's time you and Chris came home tah roost."

Abby realized she was wiping away a tear. "You know, I'd do anything for you," she said.

"Honey, what are you up to this comin' Satahday night? Mahk and I haven't had time to ahselves for so long I can taste it. Any chance you can come ovah and sit the kids, or take them out on one of your naytchah walks? They'd be thrilled. Bring Chris along. Maybe he'll take the hint."

"It's the least I could do, Rhonda. You got it."

8

When Fiorelli arrived back home, she sat down at the kitchen table and resumed her perusal of the *Globe* before opening up the latest edition of the *Cape Cod Times*. There was a story about a humpback whale stranding in Truro, and another documenting the appearance of a great white shark just off of Lighthouse Beach in Chatham.

After a perfunctory attempt at the week's crossword puzzle, Abby browsed the transaction ads and classifieds. While the news reports painted an overall picture of goings-on in the region, the transaction ads, she thought, revealed something deeper: expressions of what the locals valued, their desires and quirks, their fetishes and dark sides.

Skimming through the usual lonely-hearts ads, most of which consisted of some variation on the theme of *she/he seeks a soulmate who is a perfect match for an imperfect person*, Abby saw something that caused her to draw a quick breath and sit up in her seat. A small ad in simple block lettering read *Artemis: 7/13/8*. It couldn't possibly be a coincidence… but what could it mean?

Studying the ads more carefully, Abby discovered another brief line: *Artemisians, Nauset*. She booted up her laptop and called up a map of the Cape. After scanning the street names, she found it: Nauset Road in Eastham.

Part of the message was clearly a date: July 13. *That's tomorrow!* Abby thought. *But what about the 8? It must be the time: 8 a.m. or 8 p.m. Evening, most likely, since the daylight will be fading by then at this time of year. But who, exactly, are the Artemisians?*

Fiorelli recalled from her junior high school literature class that Artemis was also known to the Romans as Diana. She was the daughter of Zeus, and Apollo's twin sister. When Abby searched *Artemis* online, sifting through the usual litany of articles and New Age websites devoted to the latest deity of the week, she came across a page referencing *Artemisian*, a name that evokes the spirit of Artemis. And there was that symbol again: a pair of crescent moons flanking an arrow. Fiorelli dialed Roger Lemieux's cell phone.

"Hello," came a tired, familiar voice.

"Roger, it's me, Abby."

"What is this, payback for my call the other night?"

"No, and I'm sorry it's so late, but I found something in today's *Cape Cod Times* that I'm certain is a clue in this case."

"Which case is that, Fiorelli?"

"Don't yank my chain, Roger. Meet me in the morning at The Blue Plate, seven o'clock sharp. If we move fast, we could have a chance of discovering where the perpetrators are meeting tomorrow night…and maybe what the Artemisians are all about."

"Who the hell are the Artemisians?"

"Meet me at seven, Roger, and I'll fill you in."

⁓

Fɪᴏʀᴇʟʟɪ ᴡᴀs ᴀʟʀᴇᴀᴅʏ ʜᴀʟғᴡᴀʏ through her first cup of coffee when Roger walked through the door of The Blue Plate.

"Hey, Rodjah," someone called out. "Yaw girlfriend is waitin' faw yah."

"Billy," said Roger, "Don't you have anything better to do than warm up that seat? It's not like the world would fall apart if you actually got up and did some work for a change."

Sitting down across from Fiorelli, Lemieux caught the waitress's eye and pointed toward Abby's cup. She took their orders when she brought Roger his coffee.

"This is on me, Roger," said Abby.

"Thanks, Fiorelli. Now, what have you got? Judging from that call last night, I figure it's something good."

"Have you ever heard of Artemis?"

Lemieux's coffee cup paused on the way to his mouth. He stared at Fiorelli. "Yeah, that's one of those Greek goddesses, if I remember my sixth-grade mythology."

"Right. Artemis is the goddess of the hunt and wild animals. She's fierce, and an excellent shot with a bow and arrow. In Roman mythology, she's known as Diana. She often takes the form of a doe. In one story, after she is captured by the hunters, she turns them all into stags."

"You called me in the middle of the night so I would meet you here to bone up on Greek and Roman myths?"

"Last night, I was reading through the personals in the *Cape Cod Times*."

"Fiorelli, if you need to be reading the personals, what hope is there for the rest of us?"

Ignoring Roger's comment, Abby replied, "This has direct bearing on the case you brought me into. Do you want to hear it or not?"

"Okay, okay. Sorry. Don't turn me into a stag, already."

"One of the personals read simply *Artemis: 7/13/8*. A few columns over, there was another ad: *Artemisians, Nauset*. It couldn't possibly be a coincidence."

"I don't get it," said Lemieux. "How does this relate to the case?"

"I'll show you," replied Fiorelli, sliding an index card across the table. On it, she had drawn the symbol for Artemis.

Lemieux turned the card around. Jaw agape, he stared at the image, then instinctively closed his mouth and covered it with his hand.

"What the hell, Fiorelli?" he asked under his breath. "Is this for real?"

Abby shook her head, replying in a near whisper, "Yes. That pendant we found at the crime scene is a symbol of Artemis: two crescent moons on either side of an arrow. The curve of the crescent moon represents her bow."

"And what about the *7/13/8?* Obviously it's today's date, but the *8?*"

"I think it's referring to a time: eight o'clock. Since it's starting to get dark at eight at this time of year, I assume it means eight p.m."

"Right, I follow. And *Nauset* could refer to the meeting place?"

"Picture someplace that's dark and quiet."

"You mean like the end of Nauset Beach Road?"

"Exactly."

Lemieux ran his right hand over his jaw as he contemplated Fiorelli's discovery.

"This is great work, Abby. It could be the break we're looking for."

"Let's hope it is. We need to find something to tie these sickos to the crime scene. Have you had any luck tracking down their make of tire?"

"It's amazing what our databases contain nowadays. Back in my day on the force, we had to create our own sketches of different tire types. They changed the tread patterns all the time, so it was difficult to keep up."

Fiorelli smiled. "So, you had to keep reinventing the wheel?"

Try as he might to keep a straight face, Lemieux couldn't help but smile as he stared across the table at Abby. "Did you get any sleep last night?"

"I couldn't help it, Roger. That's exactly the kind of line my father would have come up with."

"It's alright, Fiorelli. Usually, your jokes aren't half bad. But that pun was a little, well...."

"Tired?"

"No...flat. Fiorelli, what does it mean when people start completing each other's punchlines?"

"I don't want to go there, but I can think of something my father might have said about the Artemisians."

"What's that?"

"It's a quote from Galatians 6:8. 'For he that soweth to his flesh shall of the flesh reap corruption.'"

"Geez, Fiorelli. I'm glad you're on our side."

"Did you discover anything about the tire tracks?"

"We're lucky. That tread pattern belongs to a very high-end make of Pirelli tire that only comes stock on a handful of vehicles. Just as you surmised, most folks who can afford cars like that simply replace their cars before the tires wear out. Or they install new tires of the exact same type."

"So, which cars does this kind of tire come on?"

"I also checked on the width of the tread we measured. That narrowed things down even more, to two models of SUV. Our suspect was driving either a Mercedes SUV, the kind with a third seat facing the rear...or, believe it or not, Jaguar now makes an SUV that uses that kind of Pirelli."

"But I thought Jaguar made sportscars."

"They still make sportscars, but ever since the company was bought by a large Chinese conglomerate, they've been making models that sell for less, and have branched out into new lines that are more lucrative. They're just hurting the brand, though. Did you know that the 1966 Jaguar XKE is the only car that ever won an international award for architectural design? That was a gorgeous car."

"Roger, you probably couldn't tell Gucci from Prada, but you talk about cars the same way you describe women."

Lemieux was about to respond, but Fiorelli held up her hand and jumped in first. "No, never mind. I'm going to head that one off at the pass. Pretend I never said that."

"What?" protested Lemieux in mock indignation.

"Whatever you were about to say is a response that's hardwired into your DNA."

"I don't see any way to win this point."

As if to put the repost out of its misery, Fiorelli stated, "There's only one way to find out what we're dealing with here. We've got to drive over to Nauset Beach Road tonight and see what we can find. If there's a group meeting of some sort, there will be cars and lights. That's a pretty desolate place after dark."

"Are you thinking there's some kind of threat here?"

"I have no idea, but I'm not about to take any chances. If this gathering is related to what we found in the canal, who knows what these people are capable of?"

Fiorelli looked at Lemieux for what seemed like a long time. Roger could almost see her wheels turning. "Meet me in the Cape Cod National Seashore parking lot in Eastham at eight-fifteen tonight," she said. "That will give the Artemisians a chance to meet and get started before we arrive. We'll hike in toward Coast Guard Beach and see what we can find. These illicit groups like to use state or federal land for their meetings because they're less likely to draw attention. Evidence is harder to trace when the location is not associated with a private residence or business.

I'm planning to accessorize with Kevlar and a sidearm, and I suggest you do the same."

"Okay, eight-fifteen in Eastham."

"Now I've got to go get some work done on my other cases. See you then."

"Bye, Fiorelli, and...."

"And what?"

"Thanks."

As Lemieux sat finishing his coffee, he looked through the front window of the restaurant and saw a big white Mercedes SUV turning into the parking lot. The driver got out of the car, came through the door, and walked over to join a group that had just been seated. Stalling for time, Lemieux pretended to be finishing his coffee as he waited for the right moment to leave. After a while, he saw the driver get up from his seat and go into the bathroom. Lemieux paid the bill and walked briskly out into the parking lot.

Casually wandering over to the SUV, Lemieux noticed that the tires were ringed with mud. When he peered into the windshield, he saw a medallion dangling from the rearview mirror: a tiny sculpture of a beautiful woman drawing back an arrow from her bow, ready to shoot. Lemieux turned and looked through the front window of the restaurant. The driver was still missing from his table. The rest of the group was deep in conversation, oblivious to the fact that he was casing the SUV, so he risked taking a closer look. Walking slowly around the vehicle, Roger discovered a withered purple flower with a short length of stem wedged into the tight seam between the rocker panel and the fender on the Mercedes' passenger side. He gently pulled the flower loose, cupped it in his right hand, and nonchalantly affected putting both hands into his pockets. Then Lemieux memorized the plate number, got into his truck, and drove a block away. It was a Massachusetts registration; the vanity plate read ART4ALL.

Lemieux pulled over and called Fiorelli's cell.

"Hey, Roger. Long time no see."

"Abby, I think the perp and his friends are having breakfast at The Blue Plate. There's a Mercedes SUV in the parking lot, and the tires are caked with mud."

"Did you get the plate number?"

"Yeah, it's registered in Massachusetts as ART4ALL, with the number 4 in the middle. And that's not all. A little purple flower was caught in a seam at the edge of the fender, so I pocketed it. Should we make a move?"

Fiorelli paused. "No, we'll wait. If we confront them now, they'll be spooked, and will probably abandon their plans. Then we'll lose any opportunity for discovery—and our only chance to see what they're scheming for the meeting at eight tonight. Run the plate number and see what you come up with. We'll meet as planned in Eastham."

"Good thinking. I like that plan. See you tonight."

"And Roger...."

"What?"

"Bag that flower and bring it with you."

9

The rising moon was nearly full as Fiorelli cut her head-lights before turning into the Cape Cod National Seashore parking lot. Rolling slowly to a stop near the main entrance off Route 6, she chose a location where Roger would be able to see her white Range Rover as he entered without inadvertently running into it.

Abby powered her window down and listened, taking in the pungent scent of the humid night air. The mellifluous call of a gray tree frog was emanating from a nearby tree. Or was it coming from another direction? *They seem to be able to throw their voices like tiny ventriloquists*, she thought. Fiorelli loved languid summer nights like this. She reveled in long walks along the beach as the waves rolled in, glistening with a million tiny moons dancing on the crashing surf. As she pictured the last time she had taken such a walk, a sentiment from one of the entries she'd read in the journals of Ralph Waldo Emerson came to Abby's mind: "I declare, this world is so beautiful that I can hardly believe it exists."

There was a timelessness about the place that compelled Abby to want to stop the world. *Why can't human beings exist in this kind of space? Why do our lives have to be fraught with so many worries and fears? Isn't this enough?*

As that thought faded away, she heard the sound of an engine being cut as Roger rolled up beside her. His headlights were off. Glancing at her watch, Abby saw that it was precisely eight-fifteen.

As if on cue, the two quietly unlatched their car doors in unison and disembarked. Holding their handles in the open position, they pushed their doors closed while slowly releasing the handle to latch—an old surveillance trick for closing a car door quietly.

Fiorelli motioned toward a large vehicle just visible on the far side of the parking lot. Roger nodded.

"What did you find out about who's behind that registration?" she whispered.

"It's registered to a business, an international import-export firm of the same name: ART4ALL. The more we dug into it, the less we seemed to find. Best we could figure was that it's a subsidiary of some kind of larger shell company engaged in illicit overseas trading."

"That would explain how they've been able to smuggle exotic animals into the country."

"Exactly."

"Ready?" Abby asked.

"Here we go."

Both instinctively checked for their guns. Without a word, they began to make their way across the parking lot.

As they drew closer to the SUV, Lemieux motioned and

whispered, "You sure got this one right, Fiorelli. That's the SUV I saw at The Blue Plate this afternoon. The one with the Artemis pendant hanging from the rearview mirror."

"I smell smoke," commented Fiorelli.

"You mean, as in, where there's smoke, there's fire?"

"No. I smell real smoke. Can't you smell it?"

Lemieux turned his face into the wind and nodded his head.

"Let's start down the main trail," suggested Fiorelli. "The one that heads over toward the bluff. There's an old campfire ring where the path looks out over the bay."

The pair walked down along the edge of a marsh as the trail began to slowly rise toward the bluff. Passing through a stand of wizened old red cedars that cast eerie, crooked shadows in the moonlight and smelled faintly of incense, Fiorelli realized why most people were easily spooked when out in the natural world at night.

At that moment, as if to complete her thought, a screech owl let out a haunting cry of descending notes that made Roger start. After collecting himself, Lemieux leaned toward Fiorelli's ear and whispered, "What the hell was that? It sounded like ghost."

"It was a screech owl. The last time I heard one, I was out canoeing on the Quabbin Reservoir. It's one of my favorite calls, so we're pretty lucky."

"Yeah, that's just how I felt when it made my skin crawl. Lucky."

Fiorelli put her index finger up to her lips, then used it

to point. "Look, up in the distance. There's a campfire." She motioned for him to follow.

As Fiorelli and Lemieux quietly picked their way along the trail at an agonizingly slow pace, the smell of wood smoke intensified, and the muted sounds of voices wafted in on the breeze. At first glimpse, the flames seemed to be flickering, but as they drew closer, they could see that the flames were blocked out each time a dancer moved in between the two detectives and the fire. The rhythmic sounds of chanting grew louder as they approached.

"What do you think they're up to?" Fiorelli asked almost silently.

"It looks like a ritual to me, like they're worshipping some kind of spirit."

When the pair was about fifty feet away, Lemieux put up his hand to motion for them to stop. Just as he took one more step to hide behind a gnarly old oak tree, his foot came down on a branch that snapped with a loud *crack*. "Shit," he muttered beneath his breath.

Things happened fast. The fire disappeared in a hiss of steam. Footfalls quickly moved away from Fiorelli and Lemieux along the trail.

For a moment, the detectives hesitated, taking in what had just occurred. "What now?" asked Roger.

"Follow them, but keep our distance," said Fiorelli. "We have the advantage while we're in pursuit. And we're standing between them and their vehicle."

"Advantage wasn't exactly on the tip of my tongue, but you're right. Let's go."

Keeping just close enough so they could hear footsteps in the distance, Fiorelli and Lemieux followed Doane Rock Trail toward Coast Guard Beach. After a time, they could hear footsteps pounding across the wooden walkway that crossed the marsh, so they knew the group was about to emerge from the brush by the Coast Guard station.

Fiorelli smelled a spicy aroma. She realized that in their haste, one of the Artemisians must have run or fallen into a patch of bayberry on the side of the trail, crushing some of the leaves. As her feet hit the boardwalk, she thought of the tiny white berries and their thin waxy coating. She'd always marveled at how many berries had to be picked, and how much work it must have been to boil off and collect enough wax to make even one candle. Shaking herself mentally, she thought, *come on, Abby—focus.*

10

Lemieux and Fiorelli stopped just short of where the trail cut through the rise of the dunes and opened onto the parking lot in front of the Coast Guard House. By the light of the full moon, the building was imposing: two stories of shingles and windows capped by a third level with dormers jutting out of the roofline. On the top, Fiorelli saw a four-sided cupola with windows on all sides surrounded by a widow's walk. Backlit by the moon, its weathervane clearly revealed the silhouette of a sailboat riding the ocean waves.

"Fiorelli," whispered Lemieux, "I saw something move on the porch on the southeast side of the house. Someone is trying to hide behind one of the columns."

"What are you thinking?"

"If they have weapons, I figure they would have used them by now. I'm going to crawl across the grass, slide through the split-rail fence, and see if I can surprise whoever is on the porch. If we can get at least one of them into custody, we can learn more about what these Artemisians are up to and why. Cover me."

"I've got your back. Careful, Roger."

Fiorelli drew her weapon, clicked off the safety, and

trained its sights on the porch. Motioning toward Lemieux, she muttered, "Go."

As Lemieux crept up along the long stretch of lawn leading to the house, he could feel the evening dew seeping into his shirt. He slid between the bottom two rails of fencing and kept moving toward the far side of the porch, away from the place where the person was hiding. When he reached the structure, he crouched and began to move along its outer edge.

When Lemieux had made it about halfway along the porch, someone leapt out from behind one of the pillars, falling on him and driving him to the ground. Lemieux reached out and grabbed his assailant by the arm, dragging him down as he fell. Their fists swung wildly, striking glancing blows that bore little force at such close proximity. A left jab caught Lemieux on the right cheek. As he went down, he became aware of numerous footfalls rushing down the metal fire escape on the back side of the building. More running feet emerged from behind the small cape-like extension that was attached by an ell off the northeast side of the main house.

Watching from the perimeter of the parking lot, Fiorelli saw Lemieux creep along the edge of the porch, and then go down in a blur of motion she couldn't quite make out from such a distance. After a few minutes of scuffling sounds, Abby was about to move in to see if he needed help when she saw the group running away from the building. Advancing quickly toward it, gun trained on the porch, Abby found Lemieux just getting back onto his feet. He looked dazed.

"Roger, are you alright? Can you walk?"

"Yeah, I think I'm fine. Where'd they go?"

"They ran up Ocean View Drive toward the Nauset Lighthouse."

"Let's get after them."

"Are you up to it?"

"You mean, do I want to catch the son-of-a-bitch who just decked me?"

"Is that a pun, Roger?"

Lemieux stared at Fiorelli for a fraction of a second as if he couldn't believe what he'd just heard. "After them—before they get away!"

Bolting up the darkened road, the two had the ocean and the big night sky on their right. As Fiorelli pumped her legs, the gun holster banged against her hip and the radio she had clipped to her vest slapped at her breast. Both made it harder to keep a good pace as they gained ground along the length of Ocean View Drive.

By the time they reached the Nauset Beach Light, Lemieux and Fiorelli were totally winded. All the same, they stopped and tried to listen over the sound of their own panting to get a sense of where the Artemisians had gone.

Fiorelli glanced over at the Nauset Lighthouse. Moonlight was illuminating the dark crown where the beacon was housed, spilling over onto the white paint that covered the lower two-thirds of the tower's curved steel base. They could just make out the distant sound of footfalls.

"There," said Fiorelli, pointing up Cable Road. "They're

heading up toward the Three Sisters!" Fiorelli and Lemieux took up the chase, and didn't stop running until they had reached the head of the short trail leading into the three wooden lighthouses.

In 1989, after the structures had outlived their own obsolescence and were in danger of being undermined by erosion along the coast, they had been moved to this site and arranged in a row on a north-south axis, about 150 feet apart. The two detectives walked briskly in about fifty feet from the road, hiding behind the nearest lighthouse.

"Do you suppose they're hiding behind the other lighthouses?" Lemieux whispered. "Or maybe they've gone off into the woods?"

"I don't hear anything," replied Fiorelli, peering out from behind the lighthouse and looking across to the next. Just as her head emerged, Fiorelli heard a loud popping sound. A bullet whizzed past her left ear. Yanking her head back behind the lighthouse wall, she looked at Lemieux and murmured calmly, "Did you hear that? The bullet snapped as it passed my ear. I've never had one get that close."

"When I was in Vietnam, I had a few shots sing past my ear. That snapping sound is a kind of mini sonic boom the bullet makes as it pushes sound waves in front of it."

"Well, now we know they've got guns," said Fiorelli.

Lemieux took out his weapon, trained it on the second lighthouse, and fired off to the side. "That will draw their attention."

Fiorelli waved the end of her weapon and motioned to

the other side of the lighthouse where they were hiding. Lemieux nodded that he understood.

As Fiorelli sneaked around to look past that side, Lemieux fired another round to keep the Artemisians focused on him. When Fiorelli peered out, she was able to discern the shoulder of one of the Artemisians in the moonlight. She motioned Lemieux to join her. When he arrived at her side, she pointed. Beneath his breath, Lemieux said, "Go for the shot, Fiorelli."

"I don't want to shoot if I don't have to."

"Why the hell not?"

"I grew up playing around these old lighthouses. I love them. They're like old friends to me, and I don't want to accidentally hit one."

Lemieux stared down Fiorelli, ordering in a muted but adamant tone, "Take the damned shot, Fiorelli!"

Abby raised her gun, sighted, and squeezed the trigger, only to hear an explosive splintering right by the head of the shooter hiding behind the middle lighthouse. Someone grunted. The sounds of running footsteps were heard again, and then all was silent as the Artemisians ran past the third lighthouse and disappeared into the woods.

"Should we go after them?" asked Lemieux.

"No," responded Fiorelli. "Someone could still be waiting at the edge of the woods, just hoping for us to follow so they can get a clear shot."

"True," answered Lemieux.

After the last sounds of footfalls had faded into the night

air, Fiorelli and Lemieux stealthily made their way over to where her shot had struck the second lighthouse. A large smear of blood glistened on the splintered shingle.

"You hit him, Fiorelli. Nice work."

"Darn it, Roger, look at the bullet hole in this shingle! He must have been cut when some of the wood was blasted off. I told you this was going to happen."

"Fiorelli, don't tell me there's a kitten hiding under that tiger skin of yours."

Fiorelli didn't reply. Lemieux watched with curiosity as she tenderly ran her hand along the splintered edge of the shingle. Almost immediately, her expression steeled. "I have my evidence kit in the SUV. Once we return to the vehicles, I'm going to drive back here and take a sample of this blood for DNA profiling."

11

Slowly, the pair backed away from the lighthouse and walked toward the road, making sure to keep the building between themselves and the woods beyond. Just to be safe, they trained their weapons on the treeline.

Once they had reached the road and begun the long walk back to the parking lot, Fiorelli and Lemieux moved in silence for a time. Adrenaline pumped through their veins as the reality of what had just happened settled in. As they rounded the corner by the Nauset Light, Lemieux stopped, turned toward Fiorelli, and said, "Abby, I have to tell you. That was a great shot. And you were incredibly cool under fire."

"It's a funny thing, isn't it, Roger? You think about this kind of thing happening all the time, and hope it won't come to that. But when it does, you find that you don't react with fear. A kind of calm comes over you, and your senses lock in on that one instant in time."

"I've experienced that," Lemieux replied, "so I know what you're describing. But it's not that way for everyone, Abby. Only for the exceptional ones."

As they walked back along Ocean View Drive toward

the Coast Guard House, Fiorelli felt the brilliant blade of adrenaline melting into a warm sense of camaraderie with Lemieux—and everyone on the force with whom she'd shared moments when the action could have gone either way. Abby was grateful to have found a purpose in life which she alone was meant to fulfill. She knew it was a gift few people were privileged to receive, no matter how long they lived.

"Thank you, Roger. Hearing that from you means a lot to me." After a brief pause, Fiorelli continued, "It was even more surreal exchanging fire at a place my father and I used to visit when I was a little girl, having picnics and playing hide-and-seek behind the lighthouses."

"Maybe that's why you were so good at seeing the man hiding behind the second lighthouse."

"Maybe. Did you know that all of the Three Sisters were once active lighthouses built between 1838 and 1911? They originally stood in a row, north to south, to signal sailors that they had reached the mid-Cape."

"No, I didn't know that, Fiorelli, but I think I'm about to find out."

"Right," Abby replied. "Two of the lighthouses were situated at Chatham and the Lower Cape, and the third was at Kingsland."

"You don't say?"

"Really. And not only that…their exteriors were originally made of brick."

As Fiorelli continued with her Three Sisters story, Lemieux's smile was masked by the wan light. *If she were my daughter,* he couldn't help thinking, *I'd be the proudest father alive.*

As the detectives made their way back toward the Artemisians' campfire, Fiorelli launched into one of her signature 'nature walks,' as Lemieux liked to call them— something she often did when excited.

"Did you know that these little oaks are called *bear oak* because when we still had bears in these parts, acorns were one of their favorite foods? The Latin name is *Quercus illicifolia.* The species name means *holly-like leaf,* because that's how the leaves are shaped. These are the shortest trees in this forest. The tallest is a close relative: the scarlet oak."

"When I was a child and my parents took me swimming at Coast Guard Beach, there weren't any gray seals because they were endangered. Now, they've made such a comeback, they're a nuisance. They spend time fishing just feet from where people are swimming. Since the seals are a natural prey species for great white sharks, when the sharks come to feed, they're right in with the swimmers, and sometimes mistake a human for their prey. Surfers dressed in shiny black wetsuits can look a lot like a seal to a shark's eyes. Plus, adult gray seals can weigh 800 pounds, and they're pretty ornery—not something you'd want to mess with."

The pair strolled silently through the moonlight and shadows. "All of that said," Fiorelli reflected, "you know that I'm a scientist at heart, but looking out at this magical scene by moonlight, I can't understand how anyone could doubt there is a creative force behind all the beauty and genius in the world around us."

Looking directly and pointedly at Fiorelli, Lemieux replied, "I couldn't agree more."

12

When they reached the campsite where the Artemisians had performed their ritual, Fiorelli and Lemieux went back to their cars to get cameras, headlamps, evidence suits, gloves, and evidence bags.

"The SUV is gone," remarked Fiorelli as they returned to the parking lot.

"I was afraid it would be," said Lemieux. "It's an old trick: One perp hides off in the shadows in case anything should happen. That way, if things go wrong, there's always someone free with the car keys in hand. At some future point, the rest of the group calls the driver's mobile and gives their GPS coordinates so they can get picked up."

"So someone was watching us at the same time we were watching the Artemisians perform their ritual by the fire?"

"It would seem so."

Back at the campsite again, Lemieux and Fiorelli donned their evidence suits and gloves. They began by taking a series of photographs in landscape mode, then zeroed in to focus on the details: footprints, discarded matches, scraps of paper, beverage containers with possible DNA traces—anything the Artemisians might have left behind in their haste that could be used to construct a trail to the perpetrators.

Once they'd surveyed the scene and recorded the broad-scale evidence, the two detectives began combing for particulars. Lemieux walked over to the fire and used tweezers to pick up some scraps of meat, which he bagged. He discovered several small wet masses of green leaves, and placed them in another bag. "This could be key, Fiorelli. There are some scraps of meat left behind. Most of it has been cooked, but there are a few raw trimmings away from the fire where someone prepared the meal. I also found leaves that may have been used to make some kind of tea."

"Great finds! And Roger, come look at this."

Lemieux walked over to see that Fiorelli was holding a pink cigarette butt in a pair of tweezers. He could clearly make out the distinctive logo bearing the initials *NS*. "That's one of those Fantastics?"

"Fantasias. That's right. And where there are smokes…."

"There's fire. Now you're talking like me, Fiorelli." When Lemieux looked up, Abigail Fiorelli's smile was lighting up the night.

When the two detectives finally returned to their cars, exhausted, Fiorelli asked almost offhandedly, "By the way, do you have that flower you found on the SUV when it was parked at The Blue Plate?"

13

A few days later, Fiorelli walked into the Barnstable Police Station, feeling the singular excitement that comes from being in the flow and making connections to reveal the bigger picture in an important case.

"Good morning, Rhonda. How are you, and how are the kids?"

"I'm fine, honey. And the kids miss theyah Auntie Abby."

"So, I'm Auntie Abby now?"

"That's right. They cahn't stop tellin' everyone that theyah favorite auntie carries a gun."

"Not so sure if that's a good thing for the kids to be bragging about."

"Whether it is aw not, you should see the expressions on the faces of ah friends and relatives when the kids ah out in the backyahd playing a game of cops and robbuz with Auntie Abby as the heroine. She's always the last one standin'."

"Better than being the victim!"

"You bet yaw sweet buns."

Rhonda buzzed Fiorelli in through the main door. Abby swiped her passcard to enter the department offices. Once inside, she walked over to the forensics unit. Andrew

Coleman saw her coming and rolled his chair back from his desk. "Top o' the mornin' to yah, Abigail."

"Nice try, Andrew, but my mother was Scottish, not Irish. And even if she was Irish, she wouldn't have sounded like a leprechaun."

"You can't blame me for trying. That's what happens when a Black man tries to get all down and homey with a redheaded white girl."

"You should quit while you're behind...and, no, don't even go there," Abby said playfully, wagging her finger at him.

Andrew sat up in his chair and focused. "What can I do for you, Abby?"

"Did you get the DNA tests back yet from the campfire evidence?"

"Yes, but with mixed results. Unfortunately, we didn't find enough DNA on the cigarette butt from the campfire for the test to be conclusive. And they couldn't pull any prints from the butt or the pendant from the scene at the canal. However...and you're going to love this...I also sent samples of the tissue gathered from both sites to a forensics lab that performs species-specific DNA analysis for wildlife. They identified the tissue from the campfire as that of an ocelot, and it matches up with the remains of the ocelot Roger found in the canal."

"That's great news about the ocelot remains. It confirms what we suspected and connects the two crime scenes. I was afraid that might be the case with the cigarette at the campfire. Still, it's the same exclusive brand and style as the butt found at the first crime scene along the canal, even if that could be considered circumstantial."

Andrew broke into one of his signature smug smiles, indicating that he had another card to show. Abby looked at him and tilted her head to one side. "What?" she asked, feeling more amused than perturbed by her colleague's tell.

Andrew prolonged his pregnant silence before finally saying, "There was, however, enough DNA on the cigarette butt from the original crime scene along the canal to run a sequence." Then he sat back and waited.

"And?" implored Fiorelli, a little irked now.

"And the DNA on that first butt matched the DNA in the blood sample from the Three Sisters Lighthouse."

Now Abby broke into a broad grin. "Andrew, that's brilliant! You've confirmed the remains of the same animal at both crime scenes, and DNA from the same perp. Nice job connecting the dots." Fiorelli allowed Andrew a few moments to bask, and then, not knowing what else to say, abruptly changed the subject. "Can you imagine that kind of money…to be able to afford forty dollars for a pack of cigarettes?"

"Honestly, it's not terribly hard to imagine in this neck of the woods."

"Yeah, you're right," Abby agreed. After a long pause, she asked hesitantly, "Andrew…how do you do it?"

"Abby, I knew we were going to have this conversation at some point."

"I mean, you are so good at your job. You keep your head

down and out-perform most of the staff in this department, and still I see people regarding you as someone outside the inner circle."

"Funny you should bring this up now. The other day, when you were talking with Rhonda, I saw some of the guys standing across the room. Their eyes kept roving over toward you. I could see that they were talking about you, which isn't unusual."

"And I've seen folks staring at you, from time to time."

"Being a Black man obviously isn't the same as being a white woman working on the force, but there are some issues we both deal with, to a certain extent."

"How do you see things?"

"I mean, if you go all the way back to slavery in the South, no one ever went around stringing up women, just for being women, like they did with Blacks."

"They did hang women in Salem, though. Those women weren't witches; they were just women who had inherited property that powerful men and their families wanted to get their hands on."

"True. But they didn't get hung just because of the color of their skin."

"No, but don't you think that rape is perpetrated as much to assert power and control over women as violence is used to keep Blacks and other minorities in their 'place?' Every time I go out into the field alone, I have to watch my back."

"Abby, as a man, I really can't speak to your experience. But when I'm walking alone at night and I see a group of people coming out of a bar who are obviously three sheets to the wind, the hair on the back of my neck stands up, and my pace quickens. Racism tends to linger just about two beers beneath the surface."

Abby digested this thought for a while. "I think the thing women and POC both have to deal with on a daily basis more than anything else —when serving on the force—is the sense of being regarded as 'other,' and not one of the good ol' boys. I mean, we're fortunate to work on a force with policies that promote diversity and respect in the official sense, but attitudes are still evolving, and they have a long way to go."

"All other issues aside," said Andrew, nodding his head emphatically in agreement, "I think that's right on. I've been thinking about these issues a lot lately, what with Juneteenth being celebrated about a month ago. We had the civil rights movement in the sixties, and the Civil Rights Act. Everyone thought we were on our way. But here we are, fifty years later, with Black Lives Matter and the killing of George Floyd, right back in the thick of it. It never ends. And that's just one piece of the struggle for me personally...but that's for another day."

"How do you mean?" asked Abby.

Andrew sat in silence for a long moment as he looked Abby intensely in the eyes. Then he asked, "Just between us?"

"Absolutely," said Fiorelli, drawing her thumb and index finger across her mouth. "My lips are sealed."

Andrew got up, closed the office door, sat down again, leaned in close, and whispered. "I mean serving as a Black officer who also happens to be gay." Then he sat back and said, "But you're one of the most perceptive people I know, so I'm sure you've sussed that out by now."

Abby nodded in the affirmative, and took a moment to acknowledge and appreciate the confidence that Andrew had just shared. "It can't be easy for you, Andrew. I can only imagine what it's like. It takes a lot of courage on your part. Why did you join the force?"

"To be honest, Abby, I simply love this work. It's what I always wanted to do. But there are other reasons why I've stuck with it, despite how isolated it can feel sometimes."

"Such as?"

"I figured I could make a difference by working to change the system from the inside. Here in Barnstable, in Massachusetts, and all around the country, the jury is still out. If only civil rights were like a court case. We'd have justice when the verdict was rendered. But it doesn't work that way, and it never will. It's a process—an ongoing struggle for one small victory at a time. That's the way it is."

"I grew up on a mission in Rwanda, so I have some idea of what it feels like to be in the minority," said Fiorelli. "But a little white girl in the midst of Black society is seen as more of a novelty than a threat. I always say that there really is no way to put yourself in someone else's shoes. Our experiences are all unique, because we each see the world differently. So, I guess what I'm saying is, there's really no way for me to know what it's like to be a brother."

"I appreciate that, Abby. And I definitely have no clue

what it's like to be a sister, of any color—even more so when it comes to understanding what it's like to walk in your shoes as a woman. I got nothin'."

"See you later, sis," said Fiorelli, grinning and offering her hand to Coleman, who gladly shook it while schooling her on a traditional dignity-and-pride handshake.

"Go easy, brothah," Coleman shot back, laughing.

～

BACK AT HER DESK, Fiorelli searched crime databases for groups similar to the Artemisians. She discovered that the Artemis symbol had been adopted by a spiritualist group in Arizona whose members were convinced that by eating the flesh of an endangered species whose spirit is about to be commended to God forever, one will achieve eternal life upon one's own death. *If that twisted practice isn't the face of evil, then what could possibly be?*

Abby learned that in their rituals, the Artemisians sought an elevated plane of existence from which to commune with spirits and seek visions. They believed they could attain a higher level of awareness by drinking absinthe, a hallucinogenic substance distilled from the leaves and flowers of the namesake of their spiritual guide: *Artemisia absinthium*. For members of this highly exclusive cult, each service ended with a meal that cost $5,000 per person just to sit at the table.

Fiorelli picked up the key to the evidence file for the Artemisian case, opened her desk drawer, and took out the bag of tea-like leaves that Lemieux had gathered at the

Artemisians' campfire at the National Seashore. She brought them over to Andrew's office.

"Andrew, I think these leaves may be a link that ties this local group of fanatics to a much larger cult with global connections. Could you please check this plant tissue for the compounds found in absinthe, *Artemisia absinthium?*"

"You got it."

It seemed to take forever for Fiorelli to get caught up filling out the paperwork and the updated report on the Artemisians in addition to the other cases she was working on. The last thing she did before going home was to reach into her bag and pull out the flower Lemieux had found tucked into a body panel of the SUV at The Blue Plate. As soon as she saw it—even as withered as it now appeared, its purple color fading—she knew exactly what it was.

Purple milkweed, or *Asclepias purpurascens,* only grew in one place on the Cape: the Crane Wildlife Management area near the Otis Air National Guard base on the northern edge of Hatchville, in the traditional lands of the Mashpee Wampanoag. *I can only imagine how the Wampanoag would feel about the Artemisians' disregard for the lives of endangered species.*

At length, Abby pushed back her chair and sighed. Exhausted, she envisioned a nice meal, a walk along the dunes, and a hot bath with a glass of rosé. As she turned the key in the ignition of her Range Rover, a single thought filled her mind: *Thank the Lord it's Friday.*

14

Saturday dawned, the air glassine with fog drifting in from the sea. Abby poured a cup of coffee, sat down on the window seat, and folded her long legs beneath her. As she opened the window, the lugubrious song of a mourning dove drifted in on the cool, damp breeze. A calm settled over Abby, much like the mist pooling in the hollows of the backdune flats spread out before her...a world of their own.

"Yes," she sighed, "There is no place else I'd rather be."

Just as she was completing that thought, Abby saw the pale gray visage of a male northern harrier glide close enough that she could just make out its white rump. It came in low, as was their habit, making a lazy loop just above a stand of bayberry and seaside goldenrod. Then, as quickly as it had appeared, it was gone...a ghost from another time and place. For quite some time, Fiorelli watched the exact spot where it had vanished, wondering about how ephemeral life really was and how all the pain one endures can seem insignificant compared to fleeting moments of ecstasy.

Abby reached over and picked up one of her favorite books from the select few she kept in this hallowed spot: Henry Beston's *The Outermost House*. Often, when faced with a case that presented a stark, chilling glimpse of utter disregard for life, she found comfort in Beston's description of the daring rescue of crew members aboard the foundered *Montclair*. In this brief vignette, Beston revealed the full range of human moral character: from the crew of the Nauset Coast Guard Station, clinging dearly to a lifeline as they waded out through the raging surf in the dead of night to reach the wreck and save the two sole surviving crew, to the scavengers on shore who only saw an opportunity to gather the lathing and other useful debris, even as the spirits of the drowned were still ascending into the beyond.

Abby's mind drifted. *What if the harrier was the spirit of the ocelot coming to me out of the wreckage of this crime to show me that I am the only one who can uncover the truth—so its life will not have been lost in vain? On the other hand, how can I end up turning such a nice moment into something so dark? This job is going to….*

A knock on the door made her jump, tearing her out of the reverie. Abby turned to see Chris already coming over the threshold, all smiles, arms open wide as he crossed the floor.

Abby stood, and they embraced deeply. She clung on a little longer and harder than usual, taking the time to inhale his comforting familiarity. When her grasp loosened, Chris gently held her at arm's length, looked into her eyes, and asked, "Abby, are you okay? You look as if you've seen a ghost."

"I think I really have, but it's a long, strange story. Why don't you join me by the window, and I'll tell you about it?"

For nearly an hour, Abby leaned into the story,

emphasizing the minutia of the evidence they had found near the power plant and at the site of the campfire ritual. She recounted the scuffle at the Coast Guard House and the gunshots exchanged by the Three Sisters lighthouses.

Abby watched Chris as he listened intently to her narrative, alternately sitting upright as she described the more intense moments and leaning in with an expression of concern, taking her hands in his when she spoke of the gunfight. When she had finally finished telling the story, Abby turned to look out at the spot where she'd seen the northern harrier.

Still holding her hands, Chris asked, "What are you thinking, Abby?"

"That some people are capable of such acts of kindness, and others can be so cruel."

"And thank God for people like you, who really care. Look, you're going to catch them and put an end to this ring of twisted minds. Nice work connecting the two sites with the boutique cigarette butts and the blood on the lighthouse. It was excellent that Andrew was able to read the DNA to pinpoint the animal remains as those of an ocelot…and that flower you identified after Roger found it on the SUV at The Blue Plate? Brilliant."

Chris stood, gently pulling Abby's hands until she, too, was standing. As they held onto one another, Chris stroked the back of her head. "I don't know what I would do if something happened to you. The shots fired at the Three Sisters…well, a few inches either way…."

"Please, Chris, don't say anything more. I don't want to think about it."

Chris pulled back and looked at Abby. "I totally understand," he said, breaking into a grin. "If that bullet had strayed a little further, it might have taken out a window on the lighthouse, and then you would *really* be upset."

Abby let go of Chris and slapped him hard on the shoulder, saying, "You…you…."

"Me, what?" He took her in his arms again. "I can't believe how much I love you."

Abby looked over his shoulder, her eyebrows furrowed. "That's the first time you've ever said that you loved me."

"Didn't you know that I do?"

"Suspecting that someone loves you and hearing them say it are two different things."

"Oh, so I'm one of your suspects now?"

"Okay, that's it. Get your binoculars. It's a beautiful day, and we're going for a bird walk."

Chris strutted, birdlike, across the floor toward the front door, flapping his arms like wings.

"Honey, do you have any idea what you look like?" Abby asked.

"An ostrich?"

"No, a great big chicken."

"I'm crying fowl on that one, Abby."

Groaning, she protested, "Oh, no…don't start with the puns. It's way too early in the day."

"What happens when you hit someone with a barrage of puns before breakfast?"

Abby hesitated before reluctantly answering. "Gee, I don't know, Chris. What happens?"

"Their appetite is *toast*," he retorted, making air quotes with his fingers.

15

It was a short quarter-mile walk through the dune complex to Sandy Neck Beach. Along the trail, Abby and Chris stopped and started repeatedly, raising and lowering their binoculars at every flash in the undergrowth, calling out bird names back and forth as if playing a game of avian tennis. Abby was keeping her eye out for the harrier, but considering everything she'd been through with the ocelot case, she was delighted to simply reacquaint herself with her old familiar friends.

The nasal whine of a catbird arose from its hiding place in a patch of sweetfern, putting on the kind of energetic display birds perform when disturbed from their nests. Abby and Chris walked over to peer into a small red cedar, where they discovered a rather disheveled-looking nest of twigs amidst the aromatic scent of evergreen. As they gazed at the nest, a field sparrow called nearby. Its sweet song quickened like the motion of a bouncing ping-pong ball. When Chris pointed up toward the sky, the couple raised their field glasses to get a good look at a pair of red-tailed hawks circling overhead. Maneuvering around some overhanging poison ivy, Abby picked some tender leaves from a young sassafras tree and munched on them.

"Are they any good?" asked Chris.

"They have a kind of root beer-like flavor. I put the young leaves in salads sometimes, though when you chew them, they're mucilaginous. Did you know that sassafras is in the laurel family, and that its wood was the very first thing the colonists exported from North America back to Europe?"

"For what reason?"

"Sassafras root and bark were used for making root beer. The tea was used to help calm a fever, and to treat urinary tract infections. The Wampanoag crush the leaves and apply them directly to wounds to help prevent them from becoming infected."

"Okay, Abby, run with it. What about the berries on this red cedar?"

"They're mostly known for being used to flavor gin. Native peoples use red cedar berry tea to treat coughs and colds. It's also been used to treat diabetes. By the way, those little blue things are really cones, not berries. And it's really a juniper, *Juniperus virginiana.* And one more thing…."

"What, pray tell?"

"Red cedar is that great-smelling wood that's used to line cedar chests to keep moths away from your clothes."

"How do you know if a berry is poisonous or not?"

"I had a botany professor who used to say that in the Northeast, there is no blue berry borne by a native shrub that's poisonous. But it must be a shrub; it has to be native; and the berry has got to be blue. There are blue berries on some native herbaceous plants, such as *Clintonia*, that are poisonous. The blue berries on Virginia creeper are toxic, and the magenta berries on pokeweed are deadly. Elder has purple berries can be used to make wine and jelly, but the red berries on the yew tree contain alkaloids that paralyze the tissue in smooth muscle."

"You mean, as in the heart and diaphragm?"

"Exactly."

At that moment, a cardinal sang a series of high whistles from a pitch pine nearby. Chris and Abby looked at each other.

"Your turn," said Abby.

"Well, back when I was an undergraduate, I worked for the Audubon Society. I was in the main office one day when a frantic call came in."

"And?"

"The caller said, 'There's a pervert in my yard who's whistling at me, and he's hiding in the bushes.' So the receptionist simply replied, 'Why are you calling us? Call the police.'"

"So, what happened?"

"The same woman called back about an hour later and said the police had come and identified the perp."

"Stop making me play twenty questions. Who was it?"

"The police looked around the yard, then came to the door and told the woman she was being verbally accosted by a male cardinal."

Abby started one of her infamous belly laughs, and couldn't stop until she was wiping away tears.

Chris goaded her on. "I've got an even better one than that."

"Please," said Abby. "Tell me. God, do I need a good laugh."

"On another occasion, the same receptionist was minding the phones. She was a rather stern middle-aged woman named Genevieve from the East Side of Providence. She had a thick Brahmin accent. When she answered the phone, a woman was screaming hysterically, 'There's a bird in my toilet! When I flushed it, the bird just popped up in the bowl while I was still sitting there! What am I supposed to do?'"

"What happened?"

"Genevieve hung up on the caller, thinking it was a crank call. When the woman called again a few minutes later, Genevieve held the receiver to her chest and told the rest of us what was going on. She then held the receiver out at arm's length, inviting someone else to handle the call. I took it and got up to speed about the situation. After having her describe the bird to me, I told her, 'It sounds like you have a house sparrow in your bowl.'"

"But how did it get there?" she asked.

"Having done quite a bit of construction work, I was able to reply, 'Ma'am, the bird was probably perched on the breather pipe—that metal pipe that sticks up out of your roof. When you flush and water goes down the toilet bowl drain, the pipe lets air in to replace it so the system doesn't bind up. The house sparrow must have been sitting on the end of the vent pipe, gotten sucked into the system, and been carried along until it popped up in your toilet."

By this time, Abby was doubled over, hugging her aching stomach. "Is that story for real?"

"Absolutely. Do you want to hear the one about the squirrel?"

"No, let's save that one for another time. My abdominal muscles can't take any more!"

As they made their way silently out of the backdune scrub habitat, the couple saw a killdeer and a brilliant yellow goldfinch. Both were being serenaded by a melodious song sparrow.

"I love the call of song sparrows," remarked Chris. "In Latin, they're named for their beautiful music: *Melospiza melodia*. It literally means *song-finch melody*."

Looking through binoculars, Chris and Abby practiced their aerial swallow-spotting skills, reacquainting one another with the differences in appearance between tree swallows and bank swallows.

"Did you know that these sandy tidal blowouts make good nesting habitat for horned larks?" asked Chris.

Abby shot him a look that said *is that supposed to be news to me?*

Rising up the back of the dunes, the path cut through waving swaths of beach grass. "If I ever have a daughter," Abby stated at length, "There are some Latin names for plants I think would make a beautiful first name."

"Which ones?"

"The genus for beach grass is *Amophylla*. And for leather-leaf, it's *Chamaedaphne*. She'd probably end up with a shorter nickname, like Amy or Chammy, but the names themselves are beautiful."

Cresting the dune, Abby and Chris traversed an expansive carpet of grayish-green beach heather interlaced with the trailing vines and deep purple flowers of the beach pea.

Abby knelt down to inhale their sweet fragrance, motioning for Chris to do the same. They walked down to where a short boardwalk cut through the wispy blades of salt marsh grass bordered by high-tide bush.

The hoarse cry of a great black-backed gull mingled with the sweet high notes of piping plovers as they played a game of tag with the margins of each incoming wave. To Abby's mind, these adorable birds were going about their lives oblivious to the fact that their existence was threatened by coastal development and disturbance of their nests by hordes of beachgoers.

Well off in the distance, some fishing boats were working the bay side off Sandy Neck Beach. "This is what keeps me sane and gives my life some sense of stability," observed Abby.

"How do you mean?"

"When it comes to my work, everything is constantly changing, often from one minute to the next. I can go from a quiet afternoon of paperwork at my desk to chasing suspects bearing arms, all in the blink of an eye. When I visit the natural world, I find a constancy that's comforting and familiar. Nature is the best of best friends. She's always there for me whenever I need her. She never fails me. I can't believe how fortunate I am that my family has this house right next door to a natural area that's nearly 5,000 acres. And I'm so grateful for the foresight of the people who worked so long and hard to have Cape Cod Bay declared an Ocean Sanctuary back in the early 70s."

Chris responded with a gift that friends and lovers rarely give to one another. He listened, and didn't say a word. Little did he know what Abby was thinking: *This is what a true friend is like— someone who listens, who you can be with in silence when there is no need for words.*

The trail followed the beach for a while, so they both took off their shoes and waded into the shallows. Chris picked up something that looked like a rattlesnake's tail and held it out to Abby.

"A whelk's egg case. And here's the egg case of a skate," she continued, holding up something with four long sharp spurs that looked as if it had come from an alien planet.

When Abby and Chris reached the trail sign pointing back up into the dunes, they sat down in the sand until their feet dried. Chris reached over with his foot and ran his toe over the sensitive skin of Abby's insole.

He loved that she had the body of an athlete. Her hair was radiant in the dazzling noontime light, and he noticed that her face and arms were already burnished from long walks in the early summer sun. Her eyes reflected the jade hue of the midday sea. His heart skipped a beat.

Abby turned her gaze away from the ocean and noticed Chris looking directly at her. "What?" she asked.

"Is there any part of you that's not beautiful?"

Color rose into Abby's cheeks, flushing the soft skin above her breasts. She opened her mouth to say something, then closed it again. "Let's get out of this sun. It's getting hot out here."

"It certainly is," Chris replied, "but I don't think the sun has anything to do with it."

16

The trail climbed back over and through the dunes. As soon as they came down the other side, sinking into the deep loose sand where the beach grass had been worn away, the couple encountered a park ranger dressed in khakis. She was squatting next to an ATV, focusing intently on some upside-down milk crates.

Abby and Chris watched the ranger for a while in silence as she attended to her work. Then, as if on cue, she began to speak. "Each milk crate covers a nest of diamondback terrapin eggs, so they don't get dug up and eaten. They're our only turtle that lives in brackish water. Of every 100 eggs that hatch, just one reaches adulthood, on average. Years ago, locals caught them in large numbers and sold them to restaurants to serve as a delicacy. They were almost wiped out, and are now a threatened species. Several organizations have been working with the Town of Barnstable to bring them back. Children in the local Headstart program raise them each year and release them into the wild. In 2010, there were 122 nests located here. In 2013, there were 87 nests; in 2014, there were 152 nests; and by 2021, there were

406 nests. They're still holding their own, with a little help from their friends."

After watching for a time, Abby and Chris both thanked the ranger and headed up the trail. As they walked away, she yelled after them, "You're welcome."

"She's intense," whispered Chris into Abby's ear.

"Definitely dedicated to her work. I get that. People who love nature will do just about anything to save it."

A little further down the trail, in scrubby woodland, they came upon a barely-visible spur that headed off in the direction of the marsh. Chris took Abby's hand, leading her through some tall thick phragmites into a small sunny clearing. The secluded area overlooked a quiet bay set into the marsh's green verge. There wasn't a house in sight before them, and the phragmites created a wall behind.

Chris slid up behind Abby, slowly turned her away from him, and pulled her close. He kissed her neck and ran his tongue along the top of her spine. She felt the hairs on her neck stand on end. His hands edged down over her shoulders and settled for a time on her breasts, caressing them gently. Then his right hand slid slowly down along her abdomen until it found her inner warmth. His fingers began to move in gentle circles, and a wave of liquid amber rushed over Abby, warm and bright.

As the amplitude of his touch grew, its crest seemed as if it would collapse at any moment. Abby felt she could not sustain it, and had a vision of the arc of her own life: long, awake, and alive. She became acutely aware of the sound of a killdeer's lonely keening, the salty scent of the sea breeze, the wind in her hair, and moving with the rhythm of the undulating dune grass bending in the wind.

Chris's touch brought a clear picture to her mind: a perfect circle she'd recently seen etched into the surface of the sand by a sharp tip of dune grass, turned round and round the base of its stem by the oscillating ocean breeze. When she could hold back no longer and the wave finally crashed and released her, Abby melted back into Chris. The tension and fears of the last few days transformed into calming golden light. Tears streamed down her cheeks, gathering in a small tidepool at the base of her neck.

～

BACK AT THE COTTAGE, Abby took two wine glasses out of her mother's old china cabinet and poured some rosé for each of them. They sat down next to each other on the couch.

"In all honesty, Abby, I spend a lot of time worrying about your safety, especially after hearing about what happened at the Three Sisters lighthouses. That was an incredibly close call." Chris reached over and brushed some strands of hair from her face, dropping his hand to caress her cheek. Then he began to trace the edge of her right ear with the tip of his finger. A low groan emanated from deep within Abby's chest, encouraging him to turn and face her more fully so he could touch her other ear. "Abby, you have to promise me that you're going to be careful. If you need my help, just call my cell, and I'll be here as soon as I can."

"Thank you. That means a lot to me." She leaned over

and kissed him deeply. As they warmed to each other, their clothes fell away and their bodies began the familiar dance she knew so well. Abby was surprised to find her mind wandering to thoughts of her mother, and the way her own life had come out of a similar love between her mother and father. She wanted so much to have her own life become part of a circle of love with someone she cared for deeply.

Abby and Chris moved slowly, staring into each other's eyes. In synchronicity with a silent, timeless reading of their bodies and souls, a rush of pleasure enveloped them, and they climaxed together. When the moment subsided, Abby closed her eyes. A burning question came into her mind, hovering somewhere near the familiar cracks in the plaster ceiling above her bed. Her thoughts had turned to the same questions she'd been struggling with for the past few years. *Is Chris meant to be my true partner on this journey? If I have a child, how can I leave the house each day for work, not knowing if I am going to make it home?*

"Abby, have you drifted off somewhere?"

"No, babe, I'm right here. There's really nowhere else I'd rather be."

~

On Sunday evening, as Abby and Chris were in the midst of a long, lingering kiss goodbye, Fiorelli suddenly recalled the purple flower. She gently pulled back from him. "Excuse me. There's something important I need to give you. I can't believe I almost forgot." She went to the refrigerator, pulled out a large plastic freezer bag with the plant inside, and handed it to Chris.

"What's this sorry-looking little thing?" he asked.

"It's that purple milkweed Roger found stuck to the body of the SUV—*Asclepias purpurascens*. Could you please share it with some of your botanist colleagues at Harvard to confirm the ID? It was in such bad shape when I got it that it wasn't easy to see all of the characteristics, but I'm sure that's what it is. Purple milkweed is endangered in Massachusetts, and is only found in one place on the Cape. So this is really important, Chris."

"Absolutely. Does this mean we're now partners in crime?"

"Um, don't you mean partners in *solving* crimes?"

"Actually, after what we did today, I'm feeling kind of naughty."

"My dear," Abby replied, "the only ones who saw what we did were a couple of herons, a song sparrow, a stand of phragmites, and the wind. So if they get called to the witness stand to testify for the prosecution, I don't think we'll have much to worry about."

17

After watching the taillights of Chris's Corvette fade in the distance, Abby began to feel her spirits ebb. *Not tonight, Abby. Take care of yourself. Give Rhonda a call.* Fiorelli picked up her cell phone and pressed Rhonda's number on speed dial.

"Hey Abby, how ah yah? I thought you'd be snuggled up with Chris by now, wrestlin' with his legal *briefs*, if you know what I mean."

"Don't you mean his *long johns*?"

"Wow, Abby...I'm impressed. Where has this girl who's speakin' to me been hidin' all this time?"

"Do you think you could find a babysitter on short notice?" Abby asked her friend.

"No need. My mothah's up for the weekend. She'd be glad to have the kids to hahself for the evenin'. What did you have in mind?"

"I'm thinking of Alberto's."

"You mean that Italian place ovah in Hyannis?"

"I'll call for a reservation and pick you up about seven-ish. How's that sound?"

"Pehfect!"

~

WHEN THE TWO WOMEN walked through the front door of the restaurant, Alberto himself came over to greet them.

"*Ciao, belle!*" he exclaimed. "*Buonasera le mie bellezze.*" He looked at Abby and said, "*La bellissima Fiorelli.*" The beautiful flower. With a flourish, Alberto ushered them over to a table in a quiet corner of the room, pulled out two chairs, and gestured for them to sit. "*Siediti qui.*"

"*Come va*, Alberto?" asked Fiorelli.

"*Molto bene, grazie, Signorina Fiorelli. E tu?*"

"*Bene, bene, paisan.*"

After a few more rounds of niceties and order-taking, Rhonda remarked, "I tend to fahget that you know some Italian."

"Well, I am my father's daughter, after all. Did you know what they used to call him when he was chief of police?"

"No, but I think I'm about to find out."

"Father Fiorelli. And sometimes, to his back, the Minister of Justice."

"He must have run a pretty tight ship."

"Ohhh, yeah," said Fiorelli, raising her eyebrows and shaking her head from side to side.

After they had eaten a very full meal and were in the process of nursing a glass of wine, Rhonda sat back and stared at Fiorelli.

"What?" Abby asked, pausing the wineglass at her lips. "Did I spill something on my blouse?"

"Abby, honey, I don't know how yah do it."

"Do what? What do you mean?"

"I mean sittin' heah having a nice meal and laughin' with me one minute, or playin' with my kids like theyah favorite auntie, and then slippin' on a gun and goin' out to chase down such nasty, evil bastahds the next."

"It's my job."

"It's a hell of a lot more than that, Abby, and you know it. Yaw the strongest woman I know."

"I think I got that from my mother. She was really focused, and always told me that if I put my mind to something, there was nothing I couldn't do."

"So, what'd she say whenevah you were strugglin' with somethin'?"

"One of her favorite expressions was, 'I don't ever want to hear you say *I can't*. You've got the brains and the will, so you just keep trying until you get it right. Do you hear me, Abby?'"

After a long pause and a few sips of wine, Rhonda asked, "How old wuh you when you lost hah?"

"Eleven."

"What did you do?"

"I was only five when she first got sick. We left the mission in Rwanda and came back to Barnstable so she could get the healthcare she needed, along with support from family and friends."

"I know that, Abby. I mean, what did *you* do when you lost hah?"

Fiorelli paused for several minutes, her eyes glazing over.

"I'm sorry, honey," Rhonda said, reaching across the table and gently placing her hand on Abby's.

"It's okay, Rhon, really. At first, after she was diagnosed, my mother and I would take long walks out into the dunes, visiting some of her favorite places: the edge of the marsh where the hermit crabs live, where the sand is streaked with soil that smells of sulfur, and the high places in the dunes where the wind crests in from the sea, smelling of salt and rockweed. And her favorite place of all: the tidepool near the mouth of Scorton Creek, where it flows into the flats at low tide."

"That sounds nice, Abby."

"Yes, it was. My father was always talking about the 'beauty of creation,' and how a higher power had to be behind everything we saw."

"Well, he is a ministah."

"It was a funny thing that happened over the years as her illness progressed. I don't think my mother realized it at the time, but she and my father ended up introducing me to a friend who saved my life."

"How do yah mean?"

"Whenever I missed my mother, I would take long walks out into the dunes. There was one place in particular that felt very powerful. Sometimes, I would sit and listen to the wind, watching it move the dune grass like waves of green water. I would pound the sand as hard as I could, screaming out my anger over losing her...and *at* her for leaving me all alone. The next minute, I'd break into a smile at some silly thing she said to me, or something funny that had happened when we were baking cookies or working in the garden."

"It almost sounds like you found a friend."

"Well, not in the same way *you're* a friend, sweetie, but something different—and, if I can say this without hurting your feelings, something more."

"I ain't goin' to be jealous of some beach grass, Abby! But what do yah mean? I want to undahstand."

"In the sand and tides, the birds and grasshoppers, I found comfort that made me feel as if I had another family in nature—in the Creation my father was always talking about. He used to say that every living thing came from God, and that we're all equal in his eyes. Later on, I would learn the same thing from the Wampanoag who tend that garden over at the Plimoth Patuxet Museum. When I was in my teens, I hung out with them a lot. They were always talking about the plant people and animal people. They consider them to be part of their own families."

"You mean like the circle of life?"

"Yes, like that, but more so. After a while, I started going into nature not just when I felt sad or lonely, but also when I wanted to share something wonderful that had happened to me. Nature became my best friend that way."

Abby reached out and took Rhonda's hand to make her point. "You see, nature has always been there for me. She has never let me down. She is the best listener in the world, and nurtures me in a way that is different from what we share—not better, just different. When I was a little girl,

I used to sit completely still for hours on end, pretending that I was just another part of the natural world. I believed that if I thought that way, then the animals wouldn't even notice me."

"Did it wuhk?"

"Sometimes, yes, it did. I used to bring seeds and raisins with me. After I'd been sitting still for a long time, I'd have catbirds and chickadees come in and perch on my fingers to eat right out of my palm."

"That must have been so cool. They accepted you as one of theyah own."

"It was. A chickadee weighs next to nothing. If you take two quarters out of your wallet and hold them in your hand, that's the weight of a chickadee."

"Yeah," said Rhonda with a smirk. "I'd always thought that would be the case."

"And beauty, and sensuality—don't get me going. There's a reason that every other gift shop on the Cape is arranged to look like a shoreline scene at low tide, with all kinds of shells and herbs and soaps that smell like heather and beach pea. The mother of pearl on the inside of some shells looks like it was designed by Cartier. Have you ever seen dewdrops shining on an orb-weaver's web in the early morning light? It puts a string of pearls to shame. And the scents of salt-spray rose and bayberry have launched a thousand soaps. Then a killdeer calls, or a harrier swoops in low and close before it sees you…it just gives you the chills. Honestly, Rhonda, it's what makes me feel alive."

Rhonda leaned in toward Abby and whispered, "Is Chris waiting somewhere down in that dunegrass? Cause I have tah tell ya, if you keep on with this sensory naytchah stuff, I'm goin' to have to go somewheyah to cool off."

"I'll never tell. Let's just say that, well, you know how you can see some big waves rolling in from far away?"

"Yeah?"

"And it seems like they take a long time to come to shore, and by the time they arrive, they've grown into a huge swell before finally crashing and releasing all their energy in a spray of white foam?"

Rhonda blushed, looking around at the other tables to see if anyone else was listening. "Abby, really, I've nevah heard you go on so...you know...*graphically*. I nevah knew what Mahk and I wuh missin'. I always thought it was just a couple of sandy swells and some beach grass. You make it sound like an episode of some lurid seaside soap opera."

Abby laughed. "We could call it *The Dunes of Our Lives*."

"I've heard you talkin' about the ocean befaw, but it never sounded so...you know...hot. Is that what inspiyahd you to learn so much about naytchah?"

"Good Lord, no. I'm just teasing you, sort of. Though being outdoors with Chris does add a totally different perspective. For myself, I just can't get enough of learning about the names of plants and animals, and the fascinating things about them. And it's similar to how it is with, you know—with you as my best friend."

"You mean your best friend among we meah human

beings. Maybe I'd be more interesting if I had feathuz and laid eggs instead of givin' birth to live young. Hey, you know, that sounds like it would be a much bettah arrangement, and a hell of a lot less painful. Maybe yaw ontah somethin', Fiorelli. I'm with you, naytcha girl."

"Okay, I guess I deserved that one. I've been called everything you can imagine, including *egg-centric*. But seriously, as with nature, the more I learn about you and your children—about Alicia and Tommy and Piper—the more there is to know. Your kids are so bright, and always seem glad to see me when I visit. And they get so excited when we head down to the beach."

"That's because they really enjoy your company, and they're into all the naytcha walks you take them on. And let's face it; how many othah women do they meet who ah cops? That's some pretty majah mojo for an innocent kid. And theyah not always so nice, believe me. Honey, you don't see what happens sometimes when theyah alone togethah. It ain't pretty."

"Which reminds me. I've been meaning to ask…isn't Alicia about to turn thirteen?"

"Yeah, isn't that wild? My first baby is going to be a teenayjah!"

"Let's do something special for her, a coming-out sort of thing."

"What did you have in mind? It's not exactly like she's goin' to wanna go to a movie, oah a dance with us adults in tow."

"How about this?" asked Fiorelli, motioning with her hands around the restaurant.

"Oh, that would be pehfect. She'd love it."

"And we could have them bring out a cake and sing 'Happy Birthday.'"

"Yeah! She'll die of embarrassment and crawl undah the table! Remembah what it was like when you wuh thirteen?"

"Maybe a first 'official' glass of fine wine, then a nice chocolate dessert?"

"Now you're talkin'. But then what ah we goin' to give Alicia?"

They both burst out laughing. After a long pause and another sip of wine, Rhonda's look turned pensive. "Abby, yaw like a moduhn-day Henry Thoreau. But bettah lookin'."

"Well, Thoreau did visit Cape Cod, and he wrote a book about it."

"But theyah wuhn't any nice restaurants heah back in the 1800s!"

"No, and Thoreau didn't have much of a love life, either."

"Did he evah get married?"

"No, but he did fall in love once, with a woman named Ellen Sewall. And someone else once fell madly in love with Thoreau, but he wasn't interested...a young woman named Sophia Ford. What's fascinating is that she was also Louisa May Alcott's tutor."

"You mean, as in *Little Women*? I loved that book when I was growin' up. But what happened with Ellen, the woman Thoreau fell in love with?"

"He and his brother John both proposed to her. At first she said yes to John, but when she realized she really loved Henry, she broke things off with John. Then Henry proposed again, but Ellen's father wouldn't allow the marriage because he didn't approve of the match. He was a minister. I guess Henry didn't measure up."

"That would explain a lot about Thoreau. Maybe that's *really* why he went into the woods to be alone."

"Oh, my God, Rhonda!" gasped Fiorelli, putting her hand to her mouth.

"I'm just sayin'."

They both began to laugh really hard, starting it up again each time their eyes met until they found themselves wiping away tears.

18

Abby and Rhonda were finishing off their cup of after-dinner tea in Alberto's restaurant when Fiorelli's cell phone rang to the tune of Bach's cantata: "Jesu, Joy of Man's Desiring." Abby gave the phone a look that could kill. "I'm sorry, but I really have to take this," she said to Rhonda before reluctantly picking up the phone. "Fiorelli here."

"Hey, bro, it's yoh favorite sistah callin'."

"Hey, sistah. Whah's up?" When Abby and Andrew had finished laughing, she asked, "Seriously, what's up?"

"I was able to source a richer spot of DNA on the cigarette butt you found at the campsite over by the National Seashore."

"And?"

"And it matches up with DNA on that fancy butt that you picked up down by the power plant along the canal. This reconfirms our earlier findings that show the same perp at both sites."

"You're a genius, Andrew! You really, truly are. Just don't go telling anyone you know that I picked up someone's fancy butt in the middle of the night down by the canal."

Both exploded in laughter.

"One more thing," continued Coleman.

"What is it?"

"The little baggie you gave me that contained a substance that looked like tea…it was exactly what you thought. *Artemisia absinthium.* The tech who runs the drug forensics unit said they hadn't seen anything like that come across their event horizon in a long time, maybe never. She also said it's an extremely potent hallucinogen that causes violent behavior characterized by mania and psychosis."

"That is fantastic news, Andrew!"

"Fiorelli, you're the only person I can think of, let alone a woman, who can hear the words *psychosis* and *mania* and gets all excited because she considers them to be good news."

"Coming from someone in your line of work, Andrew, I'd consider that high praise."

They rang off.

Rhonda looked at Fiorelli and asked, "Who the hell was that?"

"It was Andrew Coleman with great news about some evidence he's been analyzing."

"Now let me get this straight," said Rhonda. "Your phone rings to the tune of a Bach cantata, and when you ansah you say hello to your *sistah*, who is really a Black man back at the police station workin' on evidence for yaw case?"

"It's kind of a long story, and I'm not really sure it would make sense if you weren't there to hear it."

"Yaw full of surprises, Abby. I'll give yah that much."

After a long pause and a few more sips of wine, during

which both women felt simultaneously pensive and light-hearted, Fiorelli picked up right where they'd left off without missing a beat.

"Seriously, Rhon, where were we? It's funny you should say that about me and Thoreau. I can't tell you how many times I've read his books, especially *Walden* and *Cape Cod*. The thing that Thoreau really understood, which I love, was the concept of living simply, with no more than we really need."

"Not so easy to do when you have three kids."

"And not when you work for the police, either. But the books I really fell in love with as a child and adolescent were written by Rachel Carson: *The Edge of the Sea* and *The Sea Around Us*."

"I'll have to get those for the kids to read."

"Please," replied Fiorelli as she reached out and touched the back of Rhonda's hand. "I'd be honored if you'd let me give them to the children."

"It would mean a lot to them, coming from theyah Auntie Abby."

"Rhonda, have you ever read Anne Morrow Lindbergh's *Gift from the Sea*? You would love that book. She wrote it during a few weeks she gave herself away from family on an island in Florida. She was there to get in touch with her inner life and see the world as a woman and mother. She writes about living simply and not getting caught up in the trappings of modern life. That book changed my life, especially the passages about love and relationships, and dealing with loss and grief. She even talks about how important it is for women to have solitude, so they can keep some sense of self and balance in their lives. And how it's hard to help or love other people if you lose touch with yourself."

"Jeez, Abby. How do you remember all these names and dates an' such? You're like that charactah with total recall in those *da Vinci Code* books."

"Not anything like that, really. But I do seem to absorb a lot of information, which really comes in handy in my line of work."

ON THE RIDE HOME, Fiorelli reflected back on a perfect day. As if to burnish the moment, a pendulous full moon appeared along the horizon above the marsh just as Abby crested the last rise before steering down the long, dark road toward home. She could clearly make out the image of the rabbit in the moon...an old Aztec legend she had learned from her father. The rabbit's head and floppy ears hung down on the right, and its fluffy tail was on the left.

Abby turned up the drive, flicked off the headlights, and walked up to the house. When she opened the screen door and saw what was hanging from the knocker, an unearthly wail rose in her throat and grew into a night-piercing scream. Abby's cry drifted out over the marsh, startling a roost of egrets in the nearby treetops and flushing them up into the darkling sky.

19

Visibly shaking, Fiorelli ran back to her car, started the engine, spun around, and floored the accelerator, wheels spraying gravel. The tires squealed when they hit the paved road, so Abby dropped her speed and took a few deep breaths, trying to calm down.

She couldn't get the image out of her mind. The few brief words she had seen on the note felt as if they were hunting her. Instinctively, she drove to the police station. Sprinting inside, she went to her office and called Roger to tell him what had happened.

"I opened the storm door," Fiorelli said in a tremulous voice, "and the ringed tail of an ocelot was hanging from the knocker. And there was a note: *Congratulations. You caught a tiger by the tail. The eye of the ocelot sees all. Now run.*"

"They must have gotten a better look at us than we realized when we cornered them over at the Three Sisters lighthouses," Lemieux replied. "Do you want me to come and pick you up?"

"No, but thank you for asking. I'll stay here at the station until I figure something out."

Abby called Rhonda next. "I'm so sorry to call you

this late, but I wonder if I can come to stay with you for a few days?"

"Of course, Abby. The kids would love it. But what's the mattah? You sound really upset."

As Fiorelli related the events of the evening to Rhonda, her nerves began to settle.

"Abby, I cahn't imagine how vulnahable you must feel right now," Rhonda said sympathetically.

"Thank you for listening. I'm feeling a little better, but I'm still pretty shaken up. On second thought, I really don't want to bring this energy into your house right now, to you or the children. I think I'd feel safer just sleeping here at the station for the night, on the cot in the staff room. Maybe I could come tomorrow?"

"It's up to you, Abby. As long as yah know yaw always welcome heah."

"Thanks, Rhonda. You're a real friend. You truly are."

"Have you told Chris what happened?"

"Not yet, but I'll call him as soon as we hang up."

Fiorelli rang off with Rhonda. Staring at the receiver in her hand, she gathered herself and dialed a third time.

Chris started out of a deep sleep, reached over to his nightstand, and fumbled momentarily with the receiver before answering in a groggy voice. "Hello? Who is it?"

"Hi, Chris. I know it's late, but something has happened."

Chris sat up on the side of the bed and switched on the bedside lamp. Urgency and concern rose in his voice. "Abby, is that you? What is it? Are you okay?"

"Well…yes…and no." For the third time, Fiorelli relayed the evening's events.

"That must have been terrifying, Abby. Let me get dressed. Do you want some company? I can come and get you."

"No, Chris, thanks. I'll be okay for tonight. I feel safe here at the station. There's a place to sleep, and I'm suddenly feeling incredibly tired. I just wanted you to know. And honestly, I don't want to go out into the night again right now."

"I understand. I mean, that makes sense after what you've been through. Are you doing alright otherwise? You're not hurt or anything?"

"No, I'm fine. Just shaken up. I can't get the image out of my mind. I'm going to make a cup of chamomile tea and read for a while until I've calmed down enough to get some sleep. I keep an overnight bag here at the station with everything I need, just in case."

"Okay. Take care of yourself, and call me if you need anything at all."

"Thanks. I will. It's going to be a long night."

20

Waking up at the station didn't leave Fiorelli any room for denying what had happened the night before. She went into the lunch room, started the coffee maker, and then immediately headed for the bathroom to freshen up. At that moment, Abby felt certain that she had never been more grateful to have stashed an overnight's worth of personal grooming supplies in the shoulder bag in her locker. Everyone teased her about the size and weight of her bag, but at times like these, she was relieved to have it with her.

Once Abby felt presentable, fortified by the warm, rich taste of the first few sips of coffee, she wandered down the hall by the offices to see if anyone had come in yet. Light was seeping out from under the door to Andrew Coleman's office. She knocked tentatively.

"Come," said Coleman, spinning around in his chair. "Fiorelli, what are you doing here so early? I didn't hear anyone else come in."

"I was already here when you arrived. It's a long story."

"Well, your timing is impeccable. I've got some solid information about the Mercedes SUV you've been trying to pin down. But what's going on? You look pale."

After Fiorelli had finished relaying the events of the previous evening, Coleman sat in silence for a time, his mouth agape.

"Abby, if they're threatening you, there's a lot more to this case than we anticipated. If there's anything I can do to support you, promise that you'll let me know."

"I will, Andrew. Thanks for offering. That means a lot to me."

"We sistahs have to stick together," he replied, radiating the broad grin that made him such a pleasure to work with.

Fiorelli smiled for the first time since she'd left Rhonda at the restaurant. "Okay," she said, gathering herself up. "What new information have you come up with?"

"There are only a handful of white Mercedes SUVs registered on the Cape in the model that comes with the tires that left the tracks down by the power plant. All of them check out fine—except for one."

"And who owns that one?"

"Some multinational conglomerate called OneStead Holdings. They're based in Hong Kong. This is the parent corporation of the import-export firm that Roger identified as the vehicle's registrant."

"So that gives us a possible connection to the endangered species market in Asia. That could be where the ocelot was smuggled from. They're captured or killed in Central or South America, then some are exported to Asia. And who knows what other endangered animals the Artemisians could be importing from the Asian market?"

"That still leaves us with a dead end here on the Cape… no pun intended. I've put out an APB on that vehicle."

"Did you run the plate?"

"Oh, you won't believe this. Here—you'll understand what I mean if I write it down for you." Coleman picked up a pen and some scrap paper and wrote: *ART4ALL*.

"What a tangled web," said Fiorelli.

"That's the idea," said Coleman. "Leave so many bread crumbs that there are multiple trails to follow. More's the chance that when you find the right trail, they'll be long gone."

"That's what puzzles me," said Fiorelli.

"What?"

"Why come back and poke us in the eye on this case by leaving an obvious piece of evidence for us to examine?"

"You mean the ocelot's tail?"

"Yes. Once the officers have finished gathering evidence at my place, please run the DNA on the tail that was hanging on my door to make sure it matches the remains we found in the Cape Cod Canal. And make sure the scene is checked for other traces, like tire tracks, cigarette butts, etc. We can't leave anything to chance or assumption."

"That'll be my top priority, once the evidence bags arrive."

"Thank you, Andrew."

Rhonda suddenly appeared, knocking on the doorframe. "Abby, I just got a call from an officah on routine patrol in Bahnstable, out in front of the cawthouse."

"What is it?"

"A white SUV fittin' the description of the cah weah

looking faw just drove right down Main Street, past the cawthouse, and is heading west on Route 6A."

21

B ack in her office, Rhonda leaned toward the microphone on her desk, pushed the SEND button, and flew
into action. Fiorelli was glad that this was happening on
Rhonda's shift. When it came to coordinating a response to
a suspect on the move, no one was quicker, cooler, or more
competent. Rhonda had spent a lifetime exploring every
nook, cranny, and side street on the Cape, so she knew the
landscape inside and out.

When she leapt into action, Rhonda became like a con-
ductor with all police stations serving as members of her
orchestra. She called in some cars to head off the SUV at the
junction of 6A, 132, and Oak Street, and at the Parker Street
intersection to keep the suspect's vehicle from veering off
Route 6A. She let up on the call button and looked at Fiorelli.
"We don't want this gettin' intah the neighbahhoods."

"Right," replied Fiorelli. "Good thinking. Let's tell all
cars to follow without escalating speed. We don't want some
innocent bystander to get hurt."

"All cahs, be on the lookout for a white Mercedes SUV
with Massachusetts license plate ART4ALL: that's Alfa,

Romeo, Tango, numbah 4, Alfa, Lima, Lima. Is anyone neah the end of Route 149? What? It's already turned ontah 149?"

"Yes," responded dispatch. "It just passed Barnstable Fire Department, but we have cars blocking the entrance ramps onto Route 6 where 149 crosses over."

"Barnstable, be awayah that the cah was just seen crossin' ovah the highway, and it's headin' towahd Mahston's Mills. Where the hell ah they goin'?"

"They just turned west on Race Lane."

"Now I see. Theyah takin' a windin' route, but generally headin' west, movin' towahd the canal while tryin' not to make it too obvious."

"Rhonda, call dispatch in Sandwich and Bourne," ordered Fiorelli. "Tell them to call every patrol car in the vicinity of the Sagamore and Bourne bridges. We need to stop all traffic moving off-Cape."

"Copy that. What a mess that's goin' tah make of the traffic along those roads."

"Yes, but no one will notice the difference!"

"Sandwich and Bourne, you have a white Mercedes SUV coming yaw way. Massachusetts plate numbah: ART4ALL, that's Alfa, Romeo, Tango, numbah 4, Alfa, Lima, Lima. Undah no circumstances is this vehicle to be allowed tah cross the Bourne or Sagamaw bridges. Move roadblocks intah place immediately to halt all traffic headin' off-Cape."

"Sandwich here. Our closest cars were here at the station. We heard your first announcement, and have already dispatched them toward the two bridges. We're also blocking the entrance ramps from Route 130 onto Route 6, just in case. But we don't have any cars left here at the station."

"Good wuhk," said Rhonda. "It's headin' right for you. It's on Fahmahsville, movin' toward Cotuit Road. As fah as we know, the occupants of the SUV should be considahd ahmed and dangerous, so we don't wanna fawce a confrontation until we can get them intah a position wheyah no one will get hurt."

"Shit!"

"What is it, Sandwich?"

"A white Mercedes SUV just drove right past the station. I can see it from my office window. And Rhonda...."

"What?"

"It looked to me like a woman was driving."

22

"Rhonda, open a channel to every police department on the Upper and Mid Cape," Fiorelli commanded.

"Done. Just push transmit, and you're live," said Rhonda, handing her the microphone.

"Everyone listen up. This is Detective Fiorelli from Barnstable. We're in pursuit of a white Mercedes SUV, plate number ART4ALL, with the 'four' being the number 4. The Bourne and Sagamore bridges are closed off, so it can't get off-Cape. This pursuit is part of a larger, ongoing case. We do not want to escalate speed, or drive the SUV into the neighborhoods. The suspects may be armed. Safety is paramount, to protect the public and to apprehend the suspect alive. The driver of the SUV appears to be a woman, and she is not speeding, so we don't want to escalate or head her off to force a confrontation. Just continue keeping a distant tail, and at the end of the day, we'll apprehend the suspect and have a chance to question her." Fiorelli heard a series of *10-4*s in response.

Rhonda turned to Fiorelli. "I cahn't believe it. It's as if the drivah of the SUV knows every move weah makin'."

"Where is it now?"

"Headin' north on Route 130 toward Sandwich."

"That means they'll pass right through the center of town. Contact Sandwich dispatch again, and ask them to radio the car that's in pursuit. Tell the driver to back off and follow from a distance going through town."

"It just turned right onto School Street," said Rhonda. "Is this some kind of game? It entahd the school pahkin' lot, circled 'round the maintenance access road behind the school, and came back out ontah School Street. Now it's goin' left ontah Main, up past the Daniel Webstah Inn. That's not good, 'cause they'll pass by the mill pond and the crosswalk everyone uses when they go tah get watah from the spring. That's a busy intuhsection."

"Is it speeding?"

"No. It just seems to be drivin' along at a normal pace. Okay, it's on Tupper Road...now it's turned up Town Neck Road...seems like it's movin' along the back roads toward the Coast Gahd station."

"Once it gets down into that bottleneck, we can block off the exit routes. Re-dispatch nearby cars toward the Coast Guard station along Gallo and Coast Guard Roads."

"Abby, I just huhd from the patrol car runnin' security down by the recreation trail. He said a white SUV just drove past the picnic table pavilion down ovah the bank, and it's movin' along the trail, pickin' up speed. People are jumpin' outtah the way. Wait...he says it just took a shahp left and flew down ovah the rocks and into the canal!"

"What?"

"That's what the officah says. Wait a minute, he's awn again. What? Abby, the cah is gone. It's undahwatah."

"Tell the officer that he is not, under any circumstances, to enter the water or take action to rescue. That water's deep and fast, and there's no way he could offer assistance without endangering his own life."

"What ah we goin' tah do?" asked Rhonda.

"The currents are incredibly strong, so we'll need to back this whole operation up and ask for rescue divers to make a salvage attempt. I'm afraid that whoever is in that car is beyond help. We won't be able to try and salvage the vehicle until the tides turn and we get a lull in the currents—and even then, there'll be just a short window to latch onto the vehicle and pull it out. Rhonda, while you're at your desk, can you look up the tide chart?"

"Showah thing, I'm already awn it. The next window would be the slack current in a little ovah three owahs from now."

"That should give us just enough time to get everything in place before then."

"Affahmative, but I don't undahstand. Why would some-one do that—take theyah own life? Faw what?"

23

Later that afternoon, the recreation trail along the Cape side of the canal was nothing like the usual quiet refuge where people usually headed to fish, walk their dogs, or stroll hand in hand. The length of the eastern end of the trail, from the power plant to Scusset Harbor, was closed to the public.

Coast Guard boats were out in the canal, diverting boat traffic around the diving area adjacent to where the SUV had plunged into the swiftly-flowing waters. Two ambulances were in place in case an emergency arose with the diving crew. A monstrous tow truck was also waiting on site—the kind used to tow semis and eighteen-wheelers when they break down on the highway.

A team of divers was donning wet suits, and assistants were helping them fasten their tanks and set the valves. Some of the divers continued talking until they had placed demand valves in their mouths to test drawing air from the tanks.

"We're looking for a white SUV that went off where these tire marks dig into the trail," said the individual who was obviously directing the action. "Visibility is low, but the vehicle is white, and it can't be very far from the point where it dropped in. These currents can reach six knots, and they're powerful enough to resist any attempt at swimming against them. But we're going in just before slack, when the tides are about to turn. The waters will be as calm as we'll get for this operation, but don't be fooled. As wide and straight as the canal appears from above, there's no end to the number of ways a diver can get into trouble once submerged: rocky ledges, years' worth of snapped and abandoned fishing lines to get caught on, and previous wrecks that haven't yet been fished out of the water, all of which we'll have to maneuver around in the murk."

"Are we going to hook onto the vehicle?"

"We're going to wrap these two wide nylon straps around the suspension behind each rear wheel, then attach the other ends to the hook on the end of the winch cable. There are three tricky aspects of this operation. One is getting down to the vehicle and wrapping the straps securely around each wheel, making sure they catch well behind the tires on the suspension so they won't slip off. The second will be guiding the cable down to the near ends of the nylon straps so they can both be hooked on. It'll take two divers to do this: one on shore guiding the cable as it plays off the winch, and the other pulling the hook down toward the free ends of the nylon straps. I want two divers working the ends of the nylon straps, one on each strap. As soon as the straps are secured to the vehicle's suspension and the hook at the end of that cable is within reach, slip the free loops on the straps over the hook. That's a total of four divers."

At that point, the supervisor signaled the winch operator

over to join them. He had been standing at the back of the truck, waiting for instructions.

Once the winch operator was standing next to the scuba divers, the supervisor continued to issue instructions, looking directly at him. "The third important mark is critical for timing on starting the winch. The four divers must *all* be out of the water and standing off to the side, away from the torque line of the winch. If any of those straps let go, or the hook slips off, or the vehicle gets caught on the rocks and resists so that tension builds up in the cable, there's the danger of a sudden release with cable, hook, and straps flying at force along the line of pull." He raised his voice and looked pointedly at everyone involved in the operation, certain to make eye contact with each individual. "If anything goes wrong, even in the slightest, signal us immediately. Once the winch puts tension into that cable, stay at least fifty feet clear on each side of the line. And one last thing: Remember there's a body in that vehicle. Prepare yourself, and don't let it distract you from the work at hand. Now, I want each one of you to give me your eyes and tell me you understand all of this. Answer me, one at a time."

In turn, the winch operator and each diver looked at the supervisor and replied, "Yes, sir."

"Good. Now, let's go fishing. By the way, this maneuver has been unofficially deemed Operation Moby Dick."

The crew smiled as they turned away and went about their tasks. Their supervisor could tell they were focused, well-trained, and pumped to be doing this kind of work.

Their jobs required them to wait patiently for a call, often seeing weeks or longer without action. Fiorelli, Lemieux, Coleman, and a small group of officers from the Barnstable and Sandwich police departments stood ready in anticipation.

"No matter how many times I've seen a salvage operation like this—and I've seen many in my day—it never ceases to amaze me how long it takes to do something that seems fairly straightforward at first glance," remarked Lemieux.

"Safety first, Roger," replied Fiorelli.

"It's not unlike any other high-tech function I perform in our systems," said Coleman. "Most of it is the prep and mindset to make sure you're going the right way, and won't end up doing more harm than good as you're working."

"What you're both engaged in right now," remarked Fiorelli, "is what psychologists call *displacement behavior.*"

"What the heck is that, Fiorelli?" asked Lemieux.

"It's when someone wants very much to do something, but isn't able to actually do it, so instead, they focus on something else that may or may not be related in order to compensate and redirect pent-up energy."

Both men looked at Fiorelli. As if on cue, they exclaimed at the same time, "What?"

Their conversation was interrupted by the sight of three divers submerging: two holding the ends of the nylon straps, and one pulling the iron hook at the end of the steel cable, which was *very* slowly spooling off the winch at the back of the tow truck.

Fiorelli didn't miss a beat. "Both of you would love to

be the ones who get to put on diving suits and go down to find that SUV, right?"

"Yes."

"But you can't, so you're going to expend that energy up here on shore talking about it, instead."

Lemieux looked at Fiorelli as if she were some kind of alien from space. "Fiorelli, do you always have thoughts like this, trying to figure out what makes other people tick?"

"Pretty much."

"Remind me to put on my lead-lined baseball cap the next time we work together so I can keep you out of my brain."

With the divers underwater, everyone's attention was devoted to watching and waiting for them to emerge. Abby, Lemieux, and Andrew stood silently. It seemed like an extremely long time before they were able to distinguish the emerging head of the diver who had pulled the cable hook underwater. He was quickly followed by the other two.

The supervisor motioned everyone off to the side, putting his hand in the air and looking at the winch operator, who nodded affirmation that he was ready. Then he lowered his hand. "Go."

At this point, the next stage of waiting began. In general, winches that pull tremendous weight—especially loads at high risk of snagging or getting hung up—move at an incredibly slow pace because the gears are set extremely low. For a while, it almost looked as if the cable was not moving at all, just vibrating. Suddenly, everyone heard the winch begin to strain as the cable was pulled taught. After several anxious moments, something gave way, and the cable started moving again.

Lemieux kept looking at it, saying, "That looks just like my line does when I'm fishing and it gets hung up on something big. That hook is either coming up with an SUV or a humongous rubber boot."

More time passed, then still more. Finally, when it seemed like nothing was changing, water upwelled near the area where the cable entered the canal as the SUV began to surface. The crushed hood eventually emerged and the white SUV slowly jerked and wobbled its way up onto the rocks, the locked wheels cuffing violently along the uneven surface. The winch operator looked over at the supervisor, who motioned his hand in a circle to signal *keep pulling*.

At last, the SUV reached the level trail along the canal. Everyone could see that there was a body slumped over in the driver's seat, its head draped in a mop of long, tangled blonde hair.

The supervisor ran his hand in a cutthroat motion. The winch operator stopped the winch, then threw off the ratchet lever and reversed the cable to provide slack. Once the hook had been removed from the nylon straps, he signaled for the others to come and take a look.

Coleman and Lemieux glanced at Fiorelli, motioning her to be the first to peer inside the vehicle. She leaned forward, careful not to touch the side of the SUV lest she disturb any evidence. At length, Abby calmly stood and declared, "This isn't a body. It's a mannequin."

"You mean, a dummy was driving that car?" asked Lemieux.

"Not on your life," Coleman responded. In an instant, he had surmised the manner in which the entire chase scene had been pulled off. "Whoever was driving that vehicle was no dummy. And he…or she…never set foot inside that car."

24

The tow truck had hauled the SUV down to the Barnstable station garage, backing up and dropping it off in the bay set up for forensics.

After the SUV had been allowed to dry for several days, Coleman and Fiorelli donned evidence suits, gloves, and masks, then began combing through the vehicle. First, they fingerprinted every surface an operator would normally touch: steering wheel, shift lever, door handles inside and out, dash surfaces, radio knobs. With their faces covered, Coleman and Fiorelli communicated mostly by motioning to each other as they examined each surface and checked it off on the vehicle evidence examination form. At one point, Coleman remarked, "I've never searched a vehicle for prints when no one was actually driving the car."

Fiorelli smiled beneath her mask. "Me neither. And I'll bet, given the sophistication of the operation we're dealing with, they were thorough in removing the prints of everyone who worked on this mastodon of a car before it led us on that high-tech wild goose chase."

The team examined the seats, dash, floormats, and other interior surfaces for any bits of evidence that may have been left lying out in the open. When all secondary forensics checks had been accounted for, they began to dig even deeper: under seats, inside the upholstery, in the spare tire well, under the hood, and within the cargo area. This was the point in every vehicle search at which Fiorelli would start asking herself just how deep they wanted to dig. She thought of the exhaustive search depicted in *The French Connection*, when the detectives dismantled an entire vehicle into its component parts and were ready to give up. Someone asked if there was any place at all left unchecked. "Just the rocker panels," a detective replied. That was where the hidden contraband was finally discovered.

Fiorelli stepped away from the vehicle and took off her mask. "Andrew, it's all in your hands now. This car had been wiped and washed clean."

"Maybe so, Abby, but this isn't 007's Aston Martin or *Mission Impossible*, where the electronics self-destruct and go up in a puff of smoke after they've done their job. Everything I need to know is waiting inside the circuit boards and mainframe computer—including, hopefully, some digital echoes of how and where the Artemisians pulled this off. Your work here is done, but mine is just beginning." With that, he reached for a tool pouch, rolled it out like a surgical kit on what was left of the passenger seat, and started dissecting the brains of the most sophisticated vehicle he'd ever worked on.

"This is what you live for, isn't it, Coleman?" queried Fiorelli.

"My heroes are Q in the 007 films and Scotty on the *USS Enterprise*. This isn't quite as difficult as trying to use a transporter to beam someone aboard while moving at warp speed, but it's still an exciting dive into new technology."

"I have no idea what language you're speaking, Andrew," replied Fiorelli, shaking her head. "And that's probably a good thing."

"So, are you implicitly calling me a geek?"

"You can sometimes sound pretty geekified."

"Look who's talking. She of the red-breasted grebe clan."

"You probably mean red-breasted merganser."

"I say grebe, you say merganser—tomato, tomahto."

"All kidding aside, you're one of the smartest people I've ever met."

"Right back at you, Fiorelli. Still, I can't tell a white oak from an aspen. To each his or her own, Abby."

"Whatever you say, sistah."

Coleman lowered his voice, leaned toward Fiorelli, and implored, "*Please* don't let anyone hear you calling me that. I'd never live it down."

"Don't worry, Rhonda's the only one who knows, and she's good at keeping secrets."

"Did you ask her to keep it a secret?"

"Not exactly."

"That's just great."

"How long do you think it will take you to glean whatever information you can from the computer?"

"It won't take long to remove the car's brains, but it

could take a few days for everything to dry out before I can retrieve the information that's stored in the computer core without erasing or somehow degrading the data as I try to examine it. Often, programmers build in self-destruct codes that garble or erase information as soon as anyone tries to access it, so I need to figure out how this system has been fail-safed *before* I try to open or read any of the files."

"I admire your patience, Andrew."

"This kind of forensics is a good metaphor for detective work in general."

"How so?"

"It involves a lot of detailed examination, and it takes a long time—all in anticipation of a breakthrough, but with no guarantees."

"And that's why we love our jobs sooo much," Abby replied, heading for the door. "Good luck, and let me know as soon as you have something to report."

"Will do, Abby. Now, go get some R&R for a change."

As she walked out the door, Fiorelli threw back over her shoulder, "May the cores be with you."

Coleman's exaggerated groan could probably be heard in the next town over.

25

F iorelli and Coleman were already in the briefing room
when Roger Lemieux walked in.

"How's retirement going, Roger?" asked Coleman.

"You're looking at it, my friend," replied Lemieux.

They reached out and shook hands in a cross between a
conventional handshake and some version of a more elaborate move that one might see between two bros: friendly
and fluid in Coleman's case, but rather awkward on the part
of Lemieux. Somewhat impatiently, Fiorelli looked over at
the two of them. Both men sat down to listen. They were
familiar with how formal and down-to-business Fiorelli
could be when leading these meetings.

"Here's the upside," said Fiorelli, pointing to places on a large
whiteboard that backed up her conclusions. "We now know that
the Artemisians are extremely wealthy, with international connections in Hong Kong. It's likely they're tapping the market
there for illicit trade in endangered species. Thanks to the
evidence collected by Roger at the Artemisians' campfire
site, and the quick work by Andrew and the techs over at the
drugs forensic unit, we have additional evidence linking our
local suspects to an international cult of Artemisians. One

of their trademarks is the use of a powerful psychotropic hallucinogen called absinthe during their ceremonies."

"So, that's been confirmed?" asked Roger.

"Affirmative," said Fiorelli. "That was a key find for you in the field, Roger, and a nice piece of research and analysis all around. Andrew, good work—and please convey our thanks to the folks in the drug lab."

"Will do. By the way, we got the DNA analysis back from the ocelot tail that was tacked to your front door."

"And?"

"A perfect match to the remains found in the canal."

"Nice work again, Andrew. Tell forensics we appreciate the fact that they moved the DNA analysis to the top of their list. I know they're backlogged for weeks out."

"Try months out," Coleman replied. "I'll let them know. Everyone likes a pat on the back once in a while."

"When they left that note on my front door along with the ocelot's tail, the Artemisians probably didn't realize—or, in their arrogance, didn't care—that they were confirming their own entanglement in one of the most lucrative and immoral markets in the world. Interpol figures that global trade in endangered species is worth some $20 billion annually. And the Convention on International Trade in Endangered Species estimates that there are hundreds of millions of transactions each year in the buying and selling of endangered plants and animals. Tigers are among the four animals at the top of the illegal endangered species trade. So are pangolins."

"I watched a show about pangolins on PBS," said Lemieux. "Along with bats, weren't they one of two suspected vectors when the COVID-19 pandemic struck, when the coronavirus leaped from animals to people—back before they developed the vaccines?" He examined the expression on Fiorelli's face, and could tell she was riding a wave of anger and indignity about this issue. He would not want to be on the other end of a gun barrel if Fiorelli caught someone red-handed in the endangered-species cookie jar. At times like this, Roger was reminded of another Italian word that would describe her passion: *fuoco*, or *fire*.

"Researchers have found that several wild animal species could have transmitted the coronavirus," Fiorelli replied curtly. "But that's not the issue."

"Then what is?" implored Lemieux.

"The issue is that wild animals belong in the wild," said Fiorelli indignantly, "not in some cage at a marketplace." She turned abruptly to Andrew, cutting Roger off before he could respond. "You said a forensic analysis of the electronics in the Mercedes SUV showed us that while the patrol cars were in pursuit, someone was sitting somewhere looking at a live map on a computer display, and could see everything that was going on. Is that correct?"

"Exactly," Coleman replied. The white Mercedes would have stood out like Moby Dick on their screen. That's probably why they chose that particular vehicle. With this kind of system, the operator could see, anticipate, and counter our every move. Whoever was working that program was able to track the movement of other vehicles while directing the Mercedes."

"Are you telling me the perps were working that Mercedes as if they were playing a video game?" asked Lemieux.

"Precisely."

"They were using some kind of joystick to move that car around in the real world, as if it were one of those self-propelled toy cars? How the hell is that possible?"

"I'd never seen this kind of technology before," replied Coleman. "It's a super-sophisticated operating program that links a remote operator to GPS coordinates and controls within the brain of the vehicle's self-driving system. This setup enables the operator to see and track the vehicle in real time via satellite view called up on a computer display, and to control the vehicle's movements. The only organizations I know of with access to software of this level of sophistication work for the military, NASA, and private aeronautics companies like SpaceX. Someone working with the Artemisians got hold of this software and adapted it so they could remotely maneuver the Mercedes SUV as if it were a Martian rover."

Fiorelli's expression was rapt. "That's amazing. The only problem is that we're not dealing with rovers moving around on a vacant planet."

"Right," agreed Lemieux. "These are not pixels on a screen, but real people on the ground."

Fiorelli motioned everyone toward the whiteboard. *Artemisians* was written at the top in large lettering. This was where she'd been recording known facts and pieces of evidence, fleshing them out over the course of the case. Abby had used markers to connect interrelated aspects in different colors: blue for possible connections, yellow for notes of interest and/or items under consideration, red for facts that still needed to be pursued, and green for known facts key to solving the case.

Coleman raised his hand. "We should also note that the Artemisians are capable of accessing cutting-edge digital technology and software programming, and have the expertise to use it."

"Right. Great point, Andrew," acknowledged Fiorelli. "Let's add that over here."

"I was on the force for over forty years," said Lemieux, "and this kind of remote-control vehicle technology feels like Pandora's box. Yikes."

"They're obviously aware of what we're doing and who we are," interjected Fiorelli, "so they must have a means of tapping into police bandwidth communications, and perhaps even hacking our phones. It didn't take them long to find my house."

"Maybe they recognized you at the Three Sisters lighthouses, as we discussed," observed Lemieux.

"I'd thought about that, too," Fiorelli responded, "but the more I considered it, the less likely it seemed. It was late dusk, and it would have been nearly impossible to distinguish faces in the crepuscular light."

Lemieux nodded in agreement. "That was exactly the

word I would have used, Detective Fiorelli," he replied with a smile. "It was right on the tip of my tongue."

"Here's what I think," said Abby, deftly sidestepping Lemieux's quip. "The Artemisians have two games going here. First, there's the perverse practice of acquiring the meat of endangered species and using it for whatever twisted purposes their cult-like gatherings are designed to accomplish. That's what we've been focusing on...until now."

Coleman raised his hand once again, and Fiorelli glanced over at him, none too pleased at being interrupted just as she was beginning to present the arc of the case.

"So," asked Coleman, "you're thinking that this episode with the SUV was not just a slipup on their part?"

Fiorelli's eyes remained fixed upon Coleman as she resumed, holding up her left hand with the pointer finger raised. "Andrew...yes. Now we have the ocelot tail hanging on my front door along with a note that says *Congratulations. You caught a tiger by the tail. The eye of the ocelot sees all. Now run.* So...activities having to do with the cult aside, the Artemisians—who are obviously well-connected, and quite likely wield considerable power in the world of business and society as CEOs, government officials, and so on—are so confident of their superiority and capabilities that they've turned this into a game of cat and mouse. It was no coincidence that we picked up the trail of the white SUV tooling right down Main Street in Barnstable. That was just the bait."

"And we're the mouse," Lemieux responded.

"Exactly," replied Fiorelli. "This fits in with the symbolism of the pendant we found near the remains of the ocelot."

"Tell me more about that," urged Coleman.

"At first glance, the pendant looks like a dagger bookended by mirror images of the crescent moon. But the dagger is really the tip of an arrow, which is a symbol of Artemis."

Coleman looked over at Lemieux. "This is going to be good."

Ignoring his comment, Fiorelli continued. "Artemis is the Greek goddess of the hunt."

"That fits with everything we've seen in this case," said Lemieux. "When I first spotted the white Mercedes in the parking lot at The Blue Plate, I saw a medallion hooked onto the rearview mirror. It was the figure of a woman holding a bow, the arrow nocked and ready to fire."

"That was Artemis. And there's even more to it than that. Artemis is also one of the iconic ancient fertility goddesses, guardian of women in childbirth."

"So you think…what?" Coleman interjected.

"That our Artemisians could be into more than just rituals of, say, consuming the meat of endangered species because of its reputed power as an aphrodisiac and a bringer of everlasting life. Somehow, I think, in their warped minds, this is also about consummation and conception."

Lemieux leaned forward in his chair. "You mean…?"

"Yes, Roger…that's exactly what I mean. When we find these pathetic, misguided cultists, there is going to be something besides meat on the table. We're talking about more than simply eating. The Artemisians are into the realm of the flesh, in the Biblical meaning of the word."

"But Abby, that brings up all kinds of possibilities," Coleman observed. "It conjures all manner of things in my imagination."

"Yes, it does," responded Fiorelli with the faintest of smiles.

"Holy shit!" exclaimed Lemieux.

26

The next morning, when Fiorelli woke up, she experienced one of those fleeting, disorienting moments when she realized that she wasn't in her own bed, but couldn't yet recall where she actually was.

One look at the stuffed toys and dolls arrayed around the room reminded her that she was sleeping in Alicia's bed at Rhonda's house. About a week ago, when she'd come to stay with Rhonda and her children, Alicia had volunteered to sleep in the same room with her little sister while Aunt Abigail was staying with them. When Fiorelli had protested and said she'd be glad to sleep on the couch, Alicia had insisted, and seemed pretty excited about the fact that Abby was going to sleep in her room.

Fiorelli waited until the morning sounds from the bathroom quieted down. When she could hear everyone downstairs preparing breakfast, she quietly slipped into the bathroom to prepare for the day. As she was brushing her teeth, she noticed that the face staring back from the mirror looked tired and haggard. "Well, what do you expect?" Abby asked her image. "You wouldn't look all bright-eyed and bushy-tailed, either, if you'd been through what I have."

A voice just outside the door asked, "Ah you okay, sweetie? I came up to ahsk if you want some breakfast. Is someone in theyah with you?"

Fiorelli saw her reflection flush. "Uh, good morning, Rhon. No, I'm fine, just talking to myself."

"No worries. I do that all the time. If I heah you arguin', then I might staht to worry. Coffee's on, if you wanna come an' join us."

"Thanks. I'll be right down."

When Fiorelli reached the bottom of the steps, she saw Alicia, Piper, and Tommy sitting at a perfectly set table with full plates of food all around. No one had eaten yet. All heads turned toward Fiorelli, who was strangely moved to tears.

Rhonda went over to her and asked, "What's the mattah, sweetie? Ah you okay?"

"Yes, I'm perfectly fine. It's just that, well, I love eating breakfast with your family. It feels wonderful."

As Fiorelli walked toward the table, Tommy got up and pulled out a chair for her, motioning her to have a seat. Fiorelli looked at him. "What a perfect gentleman." She glanced over at Rhonda, who had a big amused smile and was obviously doing all she could do to keep from laughing. "What?" Abby asked.

"Theyah waitin' fah you to staht eatin' first. They've liked havin' Auntie Abigail sleep ovah, and wanted to show yah by makin' this a very special breakfast."

As soon as Fiorelli put the first bite of pancakes into her mouth, the children began eating as if their forks had been spring-loaded. With the tension broken, Abby said, "Thank you all very much for making me such a nice breakfast. It's the sweetest thing anyone has done for me in a long time."

"You're welcome, Aunt Abigail," the children replied, almost in unison.

They ate in silence for a while before Alicia asked, "Do you like my bedroom?"

"Yes, very much, dear."

"Was the bed long enough?" inquired Piper. "I'll bet your feet hung off, 'cause you're really tall."

Fiorelli kept a straight face despite the fact that Rhonda, who was sitting opposite her at the other end of the table, was starting to lose it. "Well, Piper, Alicia's bed was very comfortable. Thank you for letting me sleep in your room, Alicia. That's very nice of you."

"Well?" Piper asked again after a long pause.

"Maybe just a little," allowed Fiorelli. "But I was perfectly comfortable."

Piper looked at Alicia. "See? I told you she was too tall for your bed."

"Okay, girls. Aunt Abigail isn't goin' tah be able tah eat hah breakfast if she's always answerin' questions."

Fiorelli glanced up and looked around the table, making eye contact with all three children. "Are you enjoying your time off from school this summer? Spending a lot of time swimming?"

Alicia replied first. "We go down to Sandy Neck Beach

a lot. I like when the tide is moving out. Then we go tubing down Scorton Creek."

"It's okay," said Tommy, "but there aren't any big waves on this side of the Cape. Mom said she'd take us swimming at Coast Guard Beach, where the waves are big enough to go bodysurfing. Right, Mom?"

"As long as we get a nice day, when theyah ahn't any rip tides. I think that would be fine."

Tommy looked sheepishly at Fiorelli. "Aunt Abigail, would you like to come bodysurfing with us? I bet you're really good at it."

Rhonda's fork stopped just shy of her mouth. She looked at Fiorelli with an expression that said *I'm sorry, but you just never know what they're going to say.*

"I think it would be fun to go to Coast Guard Beach together. And we can watch the seals there, too, while we're swimming." Abby leaned toward the children. In a conspiratorial voice, she said, "But we'd had better check the news that day to make sure there aren't any *great white sharks* in the vicinity."

"Whoah!" Tommy exclaimed. "That would be awesome." Then, turning on a dime, he asked, "What's it like being a detective?"

"Well, it's not as exciting as you might think. We spend a lot of time doing research, writing reports, and that kind of thing. It has its moments."

"Why did you want to become a detective?" asked Alicia.

"Did you know that my father was once chief of police?" Abby asked.

"No. Is that why?"

"Partly. I grew up hanging out at the police station a lot, and I guess it just kind of got into my blood."

Then Tommy asked a question Fiorelli had been anticipating for quite some time—and she was ready. "Have you ever had to fire your gun?"

"Tommy!" exclaimed Rhonda, raising her voice but trying not to yell. "I told you, we don't ask Aunt Abigail those kinds of questions."

Tommy immediately looked remorseful. "I'm sorry."

Knowing that this was a natural question for a child to wonder about, and not wanting to squelch his spirit, Fiorelli responded, "I'm okay answering, Rhonda, if it's okay with you."

"It's really up tah you, Abby. I know he's just curious."

"To answer your question, Tommy, yes, I have fired my gun; but no—and I'm sure you're wondering—I haven't shot anyone."

"When?" he pressed.

"Just recently. But the only thing I hit was a lighthouse."

With a look of complete astonishment, Tommy asked with renewed curiosity, "Why did you shoot a lighthouse?"

"Because it got in the way."

With that comment, a ripple of chuckling started around the table. It grew into a laughfest as the image floated up in everyone's imagination of Aunt Abigail shooting a lighthouse because it got in the way.

When they had all finished eating, Rhonda said, "Okay, let's cleah the table and wash the dishes. Aunt Abigail and I have tah get tah wuhk. Grandma will get heah shawtly to stay with all of yah faw the day."

"Actually, Rhon, there's one more thing before I head out. There's something I want to give to you, Piper, Tommy, and Alicia. Wait here."

Fiorelli went up to the bedroom and pulled two gifts from her overnight bag. When she came downstairs, she had two nicely-wrapped packages in her hands. "This one is for all three of you to share," she said, handing the first package to Piper. "And this is for you, Rhon."

The children unwrapped a book, and Alicia read the title aloud: *The Edge of the Sea.*

"And who is the author?"

"Rachel Carson."

Each of the children thanked Abby politely.

"But some of these words are too big for me to read," Piper observed.

"Alicia and Tommy can read it aloud," replied Fiorelli, "and soon, you'll be able to read it yourself."

Fiorelli looked over at Rhonda, who teared up when she opened her copy of Anne Morrow Lindbergh's *Gift from the Sea.* "Thanks so much, Abby."

"You're going to love it, Rhon. At some point, your

mother and I can double-team for a few days, and you can have your own excursion to the sea."

Once the dishes were cleared, Fiorelli took a cup of coffee and sat down on the couch to read the *Cape Cod Times*. Instinctively, she turned to the classified ads, only to discover another pair of messages in the personals: *Artemis: 7/25/8* and *Artemisians: Last Supper*.

Adrenaline rushed through her system. Boosted by the caffeine, it caused her hand to shake slightly. Fiorelli carefully put down her cup, picked up her cell phone, and dialed Lemieux's number. She didn't wait for a hello. "Roger, meet me at the station as soon as you can. I think we have the break we've been waiting for. I'm sorry, Rhon, I've got to go. Something critically important has come up with the case."

"Do what yah've gottah do, honey. I'll see yah at the office."

As Fiorelli was leaving, Rhon whispered, "Thanks for being so patient with them. They're so curious to know more about you. You're their hero, you really ah." Abby's friend started to tear up again.

"What is it, sweetie?"

"Theyah growin' up so fast. I love the young man that Tommy is just stahtin' to become, but I also miss the little boy that he was. And Alicia…she's already askin' about datin'. The older I get, the fastah time seems tah go by."

Abby pulled Rhonda in close. "You're doing a great job with the children. They know you love them, and that's the best gift you can possibly give."

27

When Lemieux arrived at the station, he could see that Fiorelli was already wound up. "What's happening that's so urgent?"

Abby showed Roger the ads, and he sat down slowly to ponder the obscure message. "The Artemisians are planning to have their final gathering on July twenty-fifth at eight p.m.," said Fiorelli. "That's Monday, just two days from now."

"But where?"

"Remember that purple flower?"

"Yes, what of it?"

"Well, I recognized it right away as purple milkweed, *Asclepias purpurascens*."

"Why is it always a game of twenty questions with you, Fiorelli? And what does botany have to do with our case?"

"Purple milkweed is an endangered species, and it only grows in one place on Cape Cod. I asked Chris to show it to his colleagues at Harvard to confirm the ID, just to make absolutely sure. Because it was dried out and torn, the specimen was not easy to identify. But sure enough, it's purple milkweed." At this point, she knew she was toying with Roger. She could clearly see that the game was having the intended effect on him, but it was too much fun to resist. Abby paused.

Lemieux grew impatient. "*So where does it grow, Fiorelli?*" he asked with an edge in his voice.

"On one small patch of land in Hatchville adjacent to Otis Air Force Base. That's where we need to focus our search."

Lemieux blanched and stared at Fiorelli for a long moment, his mouth slightly ajar as if he couldn't believe what he had just heard. "Where did you say?'

"Next to Otis Air Force Base."

"This can't be a coincidence, Fiorelli."

"What can't be a coincidence, Roger? Why is it always a game of twenty questions with you?"

Lemieux laughed. "Okay, you got me that time." Then his smile faded. "Right after I was hired for the Force...."

"You mean back when this was *all* still Wampanoag territory?"

"Do you want to hear this, or not?"

"Yes, go on," Abby said, smiling.

"Someone applied for a permit to build a small house of worship on some land in exactly the area you're talking about," responded Lemieux.

"Why do you remember it so well?"

"At the time, our fire marshal—an old-timer named Jeremy Case—refused to sign off on the building permit because the property owner insisted that the building have only one door, in front."

"Why?"

"He said the door of a house of worship symbolized the pearly gates to Heaven, and that there was only one way to enter—through the front door. Something about a camel passing through the eye of a needle."

"So, what happened?"

"Jeremy said that if the owner insisted on building only one door, the plans would never get approved, and no one from his congregation would be seeing Saint Peter anytime soon."

Lemieux caught the look on Fiorelli's face. He couldn't tell if it was an expression of disinterest or subtle disapproval, which he often found to be the case with Abby when even the mildest jokes were made about religion.

"And?"

"Jeremy only agreed to sign off on the building permit under one condition: A back door had to be added for escape in case of fire."

"Was the church ever built?"

"Yes, I believe it was, but the property owner was such a fanatic, and so hostile to outside visitors, I don't know if anyone ever went to inspect the final construction to see if a back door had been added."

"But someone must have done an inspection if they were issued an occupancy permit," said Fiorelli.

"I suppose so." After a long pause, Lemieux added, "What you're telling me is that at the end of the day, we may yet

track down these sickos…all because one of them accidentally caught the flower of an endangered plant in the fender
of his car?"

"Wrong," said Fiorelli.

"Why wrong?"

"Remember the Fantasia cigarette butt? It's *her* car,
not his."

28

The next day, Fiorelli and Lemieux ran a GPS on the location of the church. After a couple of clicks, they zeroed in on a small building at the end of a dirt access road.

"Here's the church," said Lemieux, indicating the rooftop of a rectangular structure tucked in between the military base and the conservation area. "After the way they baited us with the white Mercedes, it's obvious that the Artemisians have been following our every move for the past few days. But they have no idea we're now onto the location where they hold their gatherings. So it's our advantage at this point in the game—and all thanks to your purple milkweed connection."

"Look," said Fiorelli, pointing at the screen. "The church is right near the Crane Wildlife Management Area. I can see why they chose this location. It's accessible, but isolated. There's only one long driveway in, which makes it much harder for anyone to approach without being seen. Let's look at surveillance options we can act on before they meet at eight o'clock tomorrow night."

"Vehicles are out of the question. Even approaching on foot would be risky. Once we're spotted, they'd call everything off, and any chance of catching them would be gone."

"A drone could monitor goings-on at the site, but they'd have to fly low, and the noise would tip off the Artemisians. There is another option."

Lemieux said, "Okay, I'll bite. And what is that other option?"

"Satellite imagery. If we can tap into a live satellite feed, we can surveil the site between now and then, and might even be able to pick up some plate numbers."

"The resolution is that high?"

"I'm going to get Andrew."

When Fiorelli returned with Coleman in tow, she and Lemieux briefed him about the site location and when the meeting was scheduled to begin. "One of the best satellite livestreams comes from NASA," said Andrew. "Their LANCE satellite feed shows images that are updated every few hours. It's not in real time—nothing we have at this point really is—but the imagery will give you an idea of what's happening at the site leading up to the meeting, including where you can expect cars to be parked, ingress and egress movements, etcetera."

"How long will it take you to tap into that system?" asked Lemieux.

"A few minutes. I just need to log into my account and input the lat-long coordinates to pinpoint the location."

"Let's move this meeting to your office, Andrew, so we can all look at this on your big screen," suggested Fiorelli.

"No problem. I'm working on an incredibly boring,

long-overdue technical report from an old case, and this would be a nice distraction."

When Fiorelli and Lemieux joined Coleman in his office, he cleared his screen and logged into the LANCE satellite feed. A line at the top of the home page showed that LANCE was an acronym for *Land, Atmosphere Near real-time Capability for EOS*.

Coleman called up the location on Google Maps to zoom in on the building and get coordinates for the site before copying the latitude and longitude data. Then he took the LANCE site through several layers of access points, pasted the latitude and longitude numbers into the LANCE search field, and clicked enter. After the computer turned its digital wheels for a time, an incredibly clear image of the building appeared. Backed up to forestland, it was fronted by a large open green area that looked like a field. There were two cars parked in front of the building, and the group could clearly make out the top of a fairly large truck.

"You're lucky the weather forecast calls for clear skies for the next few days," remarked Coleman.

"When was this photo taken?" asked Fiorelli.

"The date stamp says it was a little over two hours ago," answered Coleman.

"They may have rented a truck to bring some things in for tomorrow evening's gathering," observed Lemieux. "I guess even sickos need to make their plans, as strange as that may seem."

"Andrew," asked Fiorelli, "can we set up a screen somewhere where I can monitor these images from time to time?"

"No problem. There's another large screen in the dispatch office that hardly ever gets used."

"Perfect. This information is going to make a huge difference as we plan for tomorrow night's move on the Artemisians."

~

BEFORE FIORELLI LEFT THE station, she rang up Chief Martin Morales to see if he was in his office. Though his management style with detectives was pretty hands-off, Fiorelli always kept him in the loop on major cases, especially ones of this magnitude.

The chief answered the phone with his usual economy of words. "Morales."

"Chief, do you have a few minutes to run through the operation we're planning tomorrow on the Artemisian case?" asked Fiorelli.

"A few—if you can stop by now, before something else hits my desk."

Fiorelli walked into Morales' office and sat down facing him. She laid out the plans they'd made so far for the operation.

"This is a big case, Fiorelli, and you're doing a hell of a job with it. Is there anything you need?"

"Yes. Lemieux is going to accompany me to the building where the Artemisians are planning to meet at eight o'clock tomorrow night. We're going to park in a well-hidden place and walk in. This is a group of wealthy, powerful, armed individuals who, I strongly suspect, will not come willingly into custody."

"So you need some real force in the backup piece of this plan."

"Absolutely. We'll have our radios, but if we could have two additional squad cars hidden no more than a quarter-mile away in addition to an ambulance on standby, that should do it."

"You got it, Fiorelli. That all makes sense to me. We want this to be as quick and clean as it can be, and there's no sense leaving anything to chance."

"Thank you, Chief."

"Anytime, Fiorelli. Anything else?"

"That's all."

"Good luck to you. And Fiorelli...."

"Yes?"

"Don't be a hero. We want you, and everyone else, to get back here safely after this raid is over."

"We'll do our best."

Morales picked up the file he'd been working on, dismissing Fiorelli with a friendly nod.

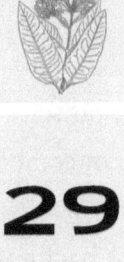

29

As the day wore on, Fiorelli could feel the tension building, and it became difficult to focus on anything else. After some mundane deskwork, she decided to take the afternoon off and get out for a long walk. With the Artemisians now focused on their next meeting, she felt safer in doing so. Besides, her wild spirit could only suffer containment for so long. When Abby returned to the cottage, she made some lunch and ate it while reading the newspaper. Moving along from one article to the next, she found herself thinking, *I can't believe reading so much bad news is somehow relaxing.*

Out on the Sandy Neck Beach trail once again, everything else seemed to fall away. Abby often visualized the concerns of any given day as layers of heavy clothing she could mentally shed, one layer at a time, as her walk progressed. After a while, the ruse took effect, and she began to feel lighter and more present in the moment.

As the trail penetrated some scrub black oak, Fiorelli noticed the glaring yellow eyes of a tiny eastern screech-owl peering from a branch and stopped short. Instead of fleeing, the bird remained where it was perched, turning its head to face Abby as she walked slowly by. Fiorelli loved screech owls, but had mixed feelings about seeing one at this particular time. She was aware that in many Native American cultures, sighting an owl, especially in daytime, was considered an omen of death.

A short distance along the trail, Abby picked and crushed a bayberry leaf to smell its spicy aroma. She was in the habit of rubbing the leaves on her arms to help repel biting insects. Then she stooped over to smell some of the reddish-purple flowers of the salt-spray rose, *Rosa rugosa*. In a few months, the branches would be full of the rose hips her mother used to pick for making jelly.

Fiorelli's mind wandered, and she felt conflicted. On one hand, this kind of leisure time in the middle of the day caused her to feel like she wasn't doing her job, but then again, she had no qualms about working 12-hour days that stretched well into the night.

These trail walks were filled with familiar, endearing sights and sounds that had, by now, worked their way into the core of Abby's being, resonating with her elemental self. Where else would she want to be to prepare her body and mind for something this unpredictable and dangerous? Abby realized that with something big on the immediate horizon, she needed to gather herself and focus. One distracted moment during this kind of operation could mean someone getting hurt or even killed. She never knew when one of these comforting visits in nature's company might end up being a final goodbye.

Fiorelli stopped at one of her favorite vantage points

overlooking the marsh: a place she had often stood as a child, holding her mother's hand. Now, she folded her hands together as if in prayer. *I know I haven't spoken to you in a while, Mom, but I love you very much. I just get so busy sometimes when I'm going from one thing to the next. Please help me find the strength to do what I have to do over the next few days. I miss you.*

Making her way back to the cottage, Abby reached the end of the long driveway, opened the mailbox, and discovered a letter from Rwanda, date-stamped two weeks previously. It carried her father's favorite postage stamp: an image of Mother Theresa.

Back at the cottage, Abby poured a glass of sparkling water, sat down on the couch, and carefully opened the letter. Her father was a man of few words and didn't write very often, but his letters, when they came, usually coincided with a significant event in her life. She was not surprised to hear from him on this particular day.

To My Little Flower:

I apologize for being so long in between letters. The usual hectic mission activities are still beyond normal, even now, some years after the coronavirus first arrived here in Rwanda and surrounding countries. Rwanda was not impacted by the number of infections other nations saw, but the lingering economic impact is still disrupting the food supply throughout Africa. I spend most of my time these days shuffling off to Kigali to meet with donors and funders to ask support for our mission, especially our efforts to keep everyone in the Nkuli region fed, hospitals supplied with medicine, and—most of all—the coronavirus vaccine.

But enough of my ramblings. How are you, my dear? I hope your work is not too taxing, and you are taking time to enjoy other aspects of your life. Are you still seeing Mr. Armstrong? If so, has he made his intentions clear to you yet? From our brief time together during my last visit, he seems like a decent, honorable man. But you know my feelings about wanting the best for you, and I hope a commitment is forthcoming.

I recently visited the Nyungwe Forest with some expert birder friends, and was treated to a rare sighting of an endangered Albertine owlet. It made me think of you and your love for the little screech owls we've encountered on our walks. Their Albertine cousin is nearly the same size.

I was hoping to come to visit you in September, but the intense demands of my work here will not allow. My sincere wish is to be able to see you for Christmas. Hopefully, you will have some news for me by then?

Baba Yako Mpendwa
Angelo

Abby put down the letter and sipped her drink. Having just seen the screech-owl, she felt goosebumps upon reading about her father's owl sighting in Rwanda. Concurrently, her concerns had only intensified with regard to what she might soon be facing in the Artemisian case. Despite her firm grounding in science, Fiorelli didn't believe such signs to be mere coincidence. Still, she was glad to hear from her father, and was reminded of the fact that during the long lapses between letters and visits, she tended to become less cognizant of the common interests the two of them shared... and how much she missed him. The usual queries about Chris and his intentions had the desired effect of prompting a prickly reaction, but Abby knew his concerns came from a place of love, and that he really did want the best for her. Still, she could decipher the thinly-veiled subtext of tacit disapproval of her premarital relations with Chris. It was, all in all, a classic letter from her father, but Abby found the reference to the Albertine owl deeply disturbing.

30

The next morning, Fiorelli was making coffee when she realized that the thing she always experienced on the morning of a big enforcement action was now happening. It was nothing she ever sought out or planned, but an internal shift hardwired into her very DNA. Abby's nerves were steeling. She was becoming calm and focused. Her team had a solid plan in place, with a backup contingency in case things escalated.

After sipping coffee on the window seat for a time, the energy driving her forward began to overtake the part of her that wanted to stay in a comfortable, relaxed space. Abby washed her cup and headed upstairs to get dressed. Her mind wandered. *Funny how they don't instruct you about what to wear to raid a gang engaged in criminal activity.* She chose a lightweight shirt that wouldn't be too hot under the Kevlar vest, and a heavier pair of jeans in case she ended up having to run through brush in the dark. At times like these, Fiorelli was especially grateful that the stationhouse was air-conditioned. She pulled her long, thick hair up into a tight bun, pinning it in place to keep it from becoming a distraction when the action began.

When she arrived at the police station, Fiorelli briefly greeted everyone on the way in, but stopped for a second to catch up with Rhonda.

"Mornin', Abby."

"Hi, Rhon. Everything okay with the kids?"

"Just fine, thanks. They cahn't stop talkin' about yaw story at the Three Sistahs lighthouses. I think you've added anothah chaptah to the long list of Aunt Abby adventures. The big question is how ah *you*? Ready faw tonight?"

"You know me. I get everything set, with little left to guesswork, and then I think of more details to make sure it all comes off as planned. It's not really over...."

"...until it's ovah. Yeah, I got that. But ah you wheyah you need and want tah be in preparation at this moment?"

"Yes...yes, I am. Can you meet us in my office at two o'clock this afternoon so we can go over the plan for the raid on the Artemisians? I'm sorry tonight's action will require you to find a sitter for the evening shift, but you're the best at what you do, and I always know we have a better chance of success when you're coordinating from this end. I've seen too many major actions flounder just because someone involved didn't have a clear picture of what was being planned. Besides, you're part of the team."

"Showah. I'll pop in at two, once I find someone to take dispatch durin' ah meetin'."

Fiorelli spent the morning working quietly in her office, answering phone messages and emails and getting caught up on paperwork. She normally found all of these activities extremely tedious, but today, they had an oddly calming effect, and offered a welcome diversion as she prepared for such a major operation. Abby called Lemieux and asked him to come to the station to go over their plan with Rhonda and everyone else who would be engaged and assisting with the raid—including patrol car and ambulance staff. As her father always said, "Leave nothing to chance."

~

WHEN EVERYONE WAS ASSEMBLED, Fiorelli started the briefing. "We need to define our timeline. It's about a twenty-minute ride between the station and staging area, but let's have all vehicles leave by six-thirty so we're waiting quietly out of sight well before any of the Artemisians start showing up. That way, they won't see any unusual activity as they're driving in. This will give them plenty of time to gather and commence whatever twisted event they're planning.

"Roger and I will wait in our vehicle until eight-thirty, then walk up the access road to scout out the best vantage point from which to surveil the activities and the layout inside the church. Then we'll move to a strategic location, use the bullhorn to announce ourselves, and tell those inside the church to come out and surrender.

"One last thing: The Artemisians have shown themselves to be proficient with highly advanced technology, and we suspect they have the capability to tap into our radio communications. We're going over this evening's plans and timeline in such fine detail now because once everyone leaves the station at six-thirty, we're going to run silent on all communications as we wait for the signal to advance. Barring any emergency, no one will engage unless Roger or I radio dispatch for backup.

"At that time, dispatch will contact all units and direct them to move in. In the meantime, no lights, no sirens, and no radios until we ask for backup. I want to hear everyone in the room state your name and say 'affirmative' to show that we're all clear on this point. Now, any questions?"

After the briefing, Fiorelli headed out for a long walk during which she ran through the various scenarios in her mind once again, reviewing the possibilities of how things could go during the raid and what she would do in response. She was well aware that the situation would be fluid, and the reactions of the Artemisians unpredictable. Mental preparation went a long way toward calming the nerves and increasing her ability to react favorably under any contingencies her team might face. The late afternoon dragged on in anticipation of what was to come.

31

At 8:15 p.m., Fiorelli and Lemieux found themselves sitting quietly in an unmarked squad car in the dimming light: near where the Artemisians were planning to meet, but well off the road and hidden from passing vehicles.

Lemieux had just polished off a sandwich and taken a sip of his coffee when he broke the silence. "You don't say much at times like this, Fiorelli. Aren't you going to eat anything?"

"I'm sorry, Roger. It's nothing personal. I find that once I'm prepared and mentally locked in, any conversation just diverts my focus, and focus is the thing I value most at times like these. I need to keep that."

"Aren't you hungry?"

"Eating dulls my senses and reaction time. Avoiding food beforehand gives me a bit of an edge. It's all part of how I prepare for an action of this magnitude. I guess some might say that I'm overcompensating in order to deal with uncertainty in a situation like the one we're about to face, but I'd rather err in that direction."

"We're different animals, Fiorelli. We really are. A good meal makes me feel fortified. And you never know when you're going to be chasing some perp on foot like we did the other night, from the Coast Guard House up along Ocean Beach Drive. I want to have all the energy I need for whatever might come up."

"Everything but the proverbial cop eating a donut," she said, teasing.

"Actually, Fiorelli…." Lemieux pulled a donut out of his cooler and held it up to show her.

At dusk, it was too dark in the car for Lemieux to see Fiorelli rolling her eyes. "On a serious note, Roger, let's move toward the edge of the woods as we approach the building. They won't be able to see us in our darks against the shadows beneath the trees."

"Sounds good."

"I'll signal with one finger for the first move. At that point, staying together, we'll slip away from the edge of the woods and take a peek through one of the windows at the back of the building so we can see the physical layout and where everyone is gathered. That will give us even more information to judge their reaction after we announce ourselves."

"What then?"

"I'll hold up two fingers for step two. At that point, I'll take the bullhorn and we'll split up, each moving to about fifty feet in front of the building, aligned with the two front corners. That way, there will be plenty of space between the front door and our location. If gunfire is exchanged, we won't get caught in our own crossfire, and they will have to deal with incoming fire from two directions."

Lemieux took a minute to envision the maneuvers as Fiorelli had described them.

"Sounds good to me, Fiorelli. I like that plan."

When Abby's watch said exactly 8:30, she looked at Lemieux. "Let's go do this thing."

32

After making their way up the drive toward the church, Fiorelli tapped Lemieux on the shoulder and held up one finger. On her cue, they crept along the margin of trees circling around behind the building. As they approached, Lemieux flagged Fiorelli's attention and pointed to the back wall. They both thought the same thing: *no door.*

Inching up to the nearest window, they noticed that it—and all other windows in their line of sight—were barred. The two detectives took a chance and leaned in far enough to get an eye on the scene inside. Fiorelli caught her breath at what she saw and reflexively put her hand over her mouth. Realizing what she'd done, she hoped that no one inside had detected the sudden movement.

The entire room appeared to be alive in luminous motion—a dance of shifting shadows cast by the flickering flames of hundreds of candles. Along one wall, a series of tables was arrayed, holding various fancy serving bowls filled with entrées.

Each of the meat dishes was marked and identified by an object hanging on the wall above the dish. In the dim light, Lemieux and Fiorelli could see—to their mutual shock, dismay, and astonishment—that staring out at the room from the wall were the heads of an ocelot, a California condor, a rhinoceros, and a grizzly bear. As nausea set in and she fought to keep bile from rising in her throat, Fiorelli felt exceedingly grateful that she hadn't eaten anything all afternoon. She could only imagine how Lemieux was managing to keep it down.

Their eyes turned to take in what was happening in the middle of the room. A large number of people were gathered in a circle, swaying and chanting in unison to the beat of a drum just out of the detectives' line of sight. Each member of the circle was wearing a loose tunic of the type worn by the ancient Greeks. Straining to see through the spaces in between the figures swaying in the circle, Fiorelli and Lemieux were presented with a surreal, nightmarish visage. Their mouths hung open as they watched. The hair on the back of Fiorelli's neck stood erect.

The circle of figures had surrounded an altar-like stone table balanced on two marble pillars. Upon it, two people dressed in tunics were locked in an unmistakable position together, moving to the same rhythm as everyone swaying around them. The vestments of the man and woman had largely slipped away. She was quite young and extraordinarily beautiful, but the man was at least late-middle-aged. She was positioned atop her rapturous partner, moving methodically, sliding up and down in a ritualistic form of intercourse.

As grotesque as the scene was, Fiorelli and Lemieux stared for a time, mesmerized by the movement of the dancers, the play of light and shadow. Finally, Fiorelli had seen enough. She tapped Lemieux on the shoulder and showed him two fingers. Slowly, they withdrew their faces from the window frame and made their way around to the front of the building. As they cleared the front wall, Fiorelli motioned to her partner, pointing him toward his prescribed watchpoint well away from one corner. They moved slowly and quietly into position.

As Fiorelli brought the bullhorn to her lips, she could feel her heart thumping in her chest. In that moment, her senses keened, and she began to take in the entire scene in minute detail: the arching sky of stars overhead, the last lingering fireflies of the season over the field, the spicy scent of damp herbs in the underbrush.

Across the way, Lemieux's heart was also drumming. *Come on, Fiorelli. What are you waiting for?!*

Finally, Fiorelli pulled the bullhorn's trigger switch and yelled in a full-throated voice, "Artemisians! This is the police. You are all under arrest. Cease what you are doing and come out with your hands up. We have you surrounded. Do not resist arrest. You have nowhere to escape." When the sound of drumming stopped from inside the building, Abby leaned in and announced with even greater authority, "I repeat: This is the police. Walk slowly out of the building with your hands up where we can see them. We are armed, and will not hesitate to shoot anyone who produces evidence of a firearm. Come out peacefully and surrender, and no one will be harmed."

Instantly, pandemonium broke out inside the building. Tunic-clad figures began to move about in panic, casting confused shadows through the barred windows. Fiorelli could see someone trying to pull a set of bars off one of the windows at the back of the building. A loud crash erupted as tables were overturned, spilling food, drink, and candles onto the floor. Someone screamed. Lemieux and Fiorelli saw a figure streak by one of the front windows with their tunic on fire. Then, in a flash, it seemed as if some incendiary of time had been cast upon the spreading flames. Everything seemed to burn at once inside the building. Frantically, the Artemisians pushed *en masse* to get out, but the doors swung inward, blocking the way. Soon, no one could escape the blockade created by the crush of bodies.

When he realized what was happening, Lemieux unholstered his radio and used an open frequency to call the vehicles lying in wait. "Emergency at the Artemisian site. The building is on fire with people trapped inside. All waiting vehicles, move in now. Use lights and sirens as needed. I repeat, all vehicles report to the planned rendezvous at once. Fire and ambulance response priority. This is a life-threatening situation. Potential mass casualties."

Fiorelli turned toward Lemieux, using the megaphone to be heard. A wail of sirens rose in the distance. "Roger, we have got to get that door down, NOW!"

Both detectives ran full bore toward the front door, but the fire was so completely engaged that the heat emanating from the burning building had formed an impenetrable wall.

Fiorelli and Lemieux tried to advance, but their inability to fight through the raging heat and their own survival instincts wrestled with an intense desire to create a means of escape for the Artemisians. As they pushed beyond the point of safety, they could smell their hair starting to singe and their skin beginning to blanche. At that moment, the moorings of the immense portico hanging over the front door—the one and only escape from the inferno inside—gave way, collapsing into a tangled mass of burning wood, rucking asphalt shingles, and jagged metal flashing. The debris irrevocably blocked the front door, which was itself now aflame.

Just as Fiorelli and Lemieux finally relented and turned away from the building to escape the searing heat, an explosion resounded, blowing out all of the windows. Abby felt a hard punch to her back as an object slammed into her right shoulder.

Once they had reached a sufficient distance from the circle of heat to turn back and face the building, Abby and Roger were powerless to do anything but watch the conflagration consume the church. The agonized screams of those burning alive echoed into the night. Lemieux ran over to Fiorelli, asking in an urgent voice, "Abby, are you all right?" Then he noticed the blood blossoming on the back of her shirt, where a piece of broken glass was protruding from her shoulder. "Damn it, Abby, you're hurt! You're bleeding!"

Fiorelli stood as still as a statue, staring at the most horrific sight she'd ever witnessed. She was awash in a bottomless feeling of helplessness and grief. Streaming down her cheeks,

Abby's tears glowed orange in the reflected firelight. For an instant, to Lemieux—who was caught up in his own shock and grief—the reds of Fiorelli's hair caught the reflections of the dancing flames, and it appeared for all the world as if her hair were on fire. He couldn't take his eyes off of her, and really wasn't sure what he was seeing in the visual confusion.

Finally, Fiorelli spoke. "And men loved darkness rather than light, because their deeds were evil."

"What's that, Fiorelli?"

Lemieux watched Abby's face, illuminated as it was by the fury of the lapping flames. The roaring column of heat was lofting a river of sparks and smoke that then spiraled up into the darkening sky. There was a look in Fiorelli's eyes he'd never seen before…a complex expression of resolve, bitterness, and remorse. When Roger finally found his voice, he said tentatively, "That sounds like it's from the Old Testament."

"No," contradicted Fiorelli. "But this is: 'For whatsoever a man soweth, that shall he also reap.'"

"Good God, Abby."

"God had nothing to do with this."

At that moment, Fiorelli's eyes rolled up into her head. The strength drained from every muscle in her body, and she collapsed like a rag doll. Lemieux reached out just in time to stop her fall, but could do nothing to halt her descent into oblivion.

33

Abby held her mother's hand as they strolled along the trail through the dunes. The sandals on her small feet were sinking deeply into the loose sand, making her work so hard to walk that it looked as if she were trudging through deep snow. The pair came to a low point at the edge of the marsh where the mud was exposed. Her mother stooped down, and Abby followed her lead.

"See all the little tracks in the mud, Abby? Do you know who made them, and who might live right here?"

"Mommy, you just told me a few days ago that hermit crabs live there. See? I remembered!"

"Hermit crabs never get very big, but they start off as tiny little things."

"And they carry their houses on their backs! Those little shells they walk around in."

"You're absolutely right, dear. And what do you think they do when they get too big for their shells?"

"I don't know, Mommy."

"No, but I'll bet you can figure it out if you think hard enough."

Abby watched a hermit crab scuttling sideways across

the mud. "When they get too big, do they have to leave their house?"

"That's right, baby. You're on the right track."

"And then they move to a bigger house?"

"What kind of house?"

"Another shell?"

Abby's mother squeezed her hand gently. "Good girl. You figured it out all on your own. If you think hard enough, there is nothing that you can't do, Abby."

The trail wound around the backside of the dunes, then climbed again in the direction of the sea. As soon as Abby and her mother crested the dune, a strong ocean breeze caught them unaware, forcing them to lean forward so they wouldn't get blown over. Abby could feel and smell the salty mist as it dampened her cheeks.

When they regained their balance, her mother paused to stare at something off in the distance, bright red hair waving in the wind. Sometimes, she would start by gazing to the north, slowly turn to face east, then continue toward the south until her vision had encompassed a sweeping arc. At some point along that curve, she knew she had looked directly at her homeland of Scotland, where she had bid goodbye to her own mother, Elspeth, such a long time ago.

In Abby's eyes, her mother's hair was what set her apart from the moms of other children she knew. When Abby was a little girl, she had asked her father what her mother's name meant. "Fiona means many things, Abby. It means *fair*, and *beautiful and full of light*—all the wonderful things your mother is." Abigail had not heard her father quite right, however, and for a long time after that, she thought her mother's name meant *hair*, because her hair was red and so much more alive than other people's.

Abby and Fiona half-walked, half-slid down the trail on the face of the dune to the shoreline. Abby watched her mother slip off her sandals, then she did the same. Her mother carried her sandals with a few fingers curled around the heel straps, so Abby held hers in exactly the same way. The two of them waded in the shallow waters, gradually making their way toward home.

"Mommy, look!" cried Abby, holding up a piece of red sea glass. "Isn't it pretty?"

"It's lovely, dear. Put it in your pocket and take it home. We can use it to make a necklace for you."

The tide was low when they reached the mouth of Scorton Creek. Abby knew exactly where her mother was going to stop along the way. Soon, they were both squatting at the edge of a tidepool, peering into the water at the magical little world that lay before them. In this low space, where the wind was calm, Abby could see her mother's reflection right next to her own. The blue sky in the tidepool accented Fiona's azure eyes.

"Look at that, Mommy!" she cried as a tiny little fish darted across. "Do you think it will live until the ocean comes back?"

"It will be just fine. The fish and the crabs and the sea-weed all live together here, and the ocean is what keeps them alive. Can you imagine how that tidepool would look if you were as small as that fish?"

"It would be like a little ocean."

"Very good, Abby. These are little oceans, and all the things that happen in the ocean also take place here, waiting for the big sea to return."

By the time Abby and her mother walked through the door of their cottage, they were both very hungry. "How would you like a piece of Spotted Dog, Abby?"

"Yes, please!" Abby loved the soda bread her mother made. The recipe came from friends who lived in Ireland. It was rich, chewy, and speckled with sweet raisins.

"Here you go, honey," Fiona said as she put the plate in front of her daughter, plunking down a jar of her homemade rose-hip jelly with a tiny little spoon sticking out of the top.

ABBY NOTICED THAT SHE was no longer seated at the table. She was back in the present day, and her perspective had shifted to high in the room, as if she were floating above her child self with her mother, who was miraculously alive. Abby was able to recall every detail of that perfect day as a cherished memory. Part of her was still in that moment, living the day with her mother. *If I'm with my mother, does this mean that I'm...?* She slipped into a gray void.

34

Lemieux drove slowly, weaving through the maze of ambulances and squad cars lining the narrow dirt access road to the site where the Artemisians' building had stood just a day ago. The flashing lights partially obscured the salmon hues of the early morning sky. His mind was weary from lack of sleep, and Fiorelli's collapse was playing over and over in his consciousness. Now, the aftertaste of too many cups of coffee lingered as the acrid smell of fire crept in through the car window.

After parking his car as close as he could, Lemieux got out and walked over to the small group focused upon Chief Morales, who had unequivocally taken control of the crime scene and was now directing the operation. As he approached the gathering of officers and emergency staff, Lemieux glanced at the blackened, smoldering rubble. There must have been twenty body bags lined up on the grass.

Andrew Coleman and Chief Morales were consulting with several of the firefighters and ambulance staff. Standing with the men was an attractive middle-aged woman with a long, dark braid that reached her waist.

Lemieux recognized her as Susan Fox, Chief of the

Mashpee Police. She was one of the many acquaintances Fiorelli had made among the Wampanoag she'd met in her youth, hanging around the garden exhibit at the Plimoth Patuxet Museum. Fiorelli often spoke of Fox with great respect, and had been thrilled when the Town of Mashpee appointed her friend as the first woman to serve as chief. Fiorelli had told Lemieux that Chief Fox's namesake in Wampanoag was *whauksis*. Indeed, Fox was renowned for her astute observations and uncanny knack for picking up the cold tracks of longstanding open cases and bringing perpetrators to justice.

"As soon as we're sure the last of the hotspots are out and there's no danger of this flaring up again, let's pull back all fire apparatus so the ambulances can drive closer to pick up the remains," ordered Morales. He noticed Lemieux approaching. "Roger, what the hell are you doing here?"

"Couldn't sleep, so I figured I may as well be here as anywhere. I don't want to interrupt, but when you're done here, I'd like to know what you've found and if you have any preliminary conclusions." Turning, Lemieux continued, "Chief Fox, it's good to see you again, though I wish it were under better circumstances."

"You as well, Roger. I am so sorry to hear about Abby. What a horrible experience for both of you. Chief Morales has filled us in on the verbal report you shared with everyone when they arrived on the scene last night. How is she doing?"

"It was awful. She just collapsed, and we couldn't revive her."

"My heart aches for her."

"I have never seen her so distraught," Lemieux remarked.

"No good can come from the desecration of life."

"Do you mean what happened to the Artemisians?"

"Yes, all those lost souls."

Sensing that Fox intended to say something more but was hesitant, Lemieux encouraged her. "And?"

"What they were doing to sacred animals…this tragic loss of human life…it is all connected."

Everyone paused to take in the meaning of Fox's words. Lemieux felt a catch in his throat when he sensed a haunting echo of the words Fiorelli had spoken right before passing out not twelve hours ago.

"Are you assuming point for this part of the investigation, since it took place in Mashpee?" Lemieux asked Fox.

"No, you and Fiorelli have been tracking this case for some time, and doing a heck of a job. I'm here to offer our department's support. Let me know if you need anything."

"Thank you, Chief Fox. We will."

Morales, impatience barely veiled, called out, "Roger, we're just finishing up." He turned to look at the faces of those gathered around him. "Are we all clear?" When he was satisfied that everyone had heard his orders, he continued, "Then make it so. We want to get the remains to the morgue without delay—that's first priority. Whatever these poor souls were engaged in last night, their remains deserve the respect we would afford to anyone deceased. Is that clear?" Again, there were nods all around as the team turned to deal with the gruesome scene before them.

Morales pulled Lemieux aside and motioned for Coleman to join them. "Roger, now that you're here, maybe you can help us to piece together some of the evidence that's not connecting. I know you've had a rough night since the fire, but there's no better time than the present, while we're here and the scene is fresh in our minds."

"Agreed."

"Before we start," said Coleman, "have you heard anything more about how Abby is doing?"

"I called the hospital this morning," Lemieux replied. "They're not allowing any visitors yet, but they said her condition is the same. She's stable but unconscious, and they're not sure why. There doesn't seem to be any head trauma or neurological damage. The surgeons were able to repair her shoulder—and thank God, no major blood vessels were involved or organs damaged. The shard of glass went in deep, but the cut was to the muscle, and it was clean."

"This is hard to take in," said Coleman, eyes glistening. "This is Abby we're talking about."

"Gentleman, let's get through this walk-through, and then we can drive over to the hospital to check in and see if there's been any change in Fiorelli's condition," suggested Morales. He ushered them toward the area where the front door of the building had once stood.

As they were walking, Lemieux asked, "Has there been

any determination with regard to why the building went up so quickly, and what caused the explosion?"

"It's just preliminary," said Coleman, "and we're not sure what started the fire in the first place, but once it accelerated, it seems to have caused several small propane tanks that were inside the building to explode. Do you have any idea what those tanks were doing there?"

Lemieux stared at Coleman with an expression of total incredulity. "Abby and I snuck around the back of the building. There was a small window that had been placed where the back door should have been. I saw a couple of grills going when we looked in through the window," said Lemieux. "But would tanks that small cause an explosion of that size?"

"It's not the size of the container, necessarily, Roger, but the resistance of the shell. Once the tanks overheated in the fire and the propane inside reached the flashpoint, those hardened steel casings would be able to contain a tremendous amount of pressure before rupturing. And the first one to go would have set off the ones next to it in a chain reaction. Two or three explosions of that magnitude could easily take down a building of this size. Did you see what started the fire?"

"When Fiorelli made the announcement over the bullhorn, everyone inside seemed to panic and started rushing around, looking for a way out. There were hundreds of candles on the tables, and some were set on chairs and shelves along the walls."

"I don't see how candles could possibly have caused the fire to spread so quickly. It's like there was some kind of accelerant."

Lemieux stared at Coleman for a time. His eyes drifted off to the side as he strained to recall what he'd seen through the window the night before. Coleman and Morales waited in silence, not wanting to interrupt his train of thought.

After a few seconds, Roger looked at each of them in turn as a realization came into focus. "Oil lamps," he said. "There were a number of glass oil lamps placed around the room. I remember now. There was at least one on a table near where they were cooking the meat."

"Why do you recall that particular detail so clearly?" asked Morales, wanting to make sure that Lemieux was certain about what he'd seen.

"Because the lamp was directly in my line of sight, just beyond where the couple was engaging in sex. I could faintly see a reflection in the globe on the lamp, which showed the back of the girl moving up and down."

"That image would definitely stick in your mind. I can already picture the scene, and I wasn't even there," said Coleman. "And there's our accelerant: lamp oil. If some of those lamps got knocked over and broken in the commotion, the oil could have ignited and acted like a torch, throwing fire across the floor."

Lemieux continued to recall the scene. "Right after people started moving, I saw someone go by the window with their tunic on fire…then another person…and then the flames just seemed to fill the window frame. It couldn't have been much more than a few minutes before the explosion."

"But Roger, what exactly did you see? Why weren't those people able to get out?" Morales asked.

"The portico collapsed, trapping them inside. And the windows were barred."

"That may not be all," suggested Coleman.

"How's that?" asked Lemieux.

"As far as we can tell by the way the hinges were placed on the part of the door frame that was still intact, it looked like the door was designed to open *into* the building."

Lemieux and Morales both stared at Coleman in disbelief.

"Why would anyone in their right mind do such a thing? And why wasn't this building inspected and up to code?"

"I've already called the head of that division, Miranda Gotlieb, to find out what they know. She wasn't too pleased to be bothered this early in the morning, but was helpful once she heard the magnitude of what had happened."

"Miranda's a good egg," said Lemieux.

Coleman continued. "She said that the changes to the building had to have been recent, since the building was inspected last September. At that time, there were no bars on the windows, the back door that had been required during the initial permitting was in place, and the front door was up to code."

"Why the hell would anyone make these changes to the building?" asked Lemieux. "This is basic fire safety. It's just common sense. You'd think someone involved would have thought of that."

Coleman interjected. "I don't think that was their priority. All recent changes indicate that the goal was to keep people from leaving the building once they were inside." He turned to face Lemieux. "When you looked through that window last night, did you see anything else that might help us here?"

Lemieux again described the otherworldly scene he and Fiorelli had encountered. When he came to describing the young woman engaged in intercourse on the altar-like platform, he paused, fixating on the memory of her appearance.

"You've already told us this, Roger," said Morales urgently. "But did you see anything else in particular? I don't mean to be short, and I know you've had a long, horrible night. I think we all have, and it's taking its toll."

"Wait. There was something else. I'm also remembering that there were a few individuals standing in the shadows who were not wearing tunics. They were holstered—they were carrying."

"So, some of those people may not have been there of their own free will?" asked Morales.

"Now that I picture the scene in this different light," said Lemieux, "and now that I'm remembering the figures in the corners of the room...they could have been guarding the action. But that brings up another aspect of this case. What's the word I'm searching for? I've got it...something insidious that goes with the feeling I got as I watched their ceremony last night, or whatever you want to call it."

"What's that?" asked Morales.

"That what I was seeing was pure, unadulterated evil."

35

Chris walked into the intensive care unit gingerly, as one would walk into a church when a service had already begun. A familiar cadence of beeps mingled with flashing lights, and the harsh antiseptic smell common to these rooms evoked in him an incongruous perception of both sickness and healing. Abigail lay still, her hands on top of the sheets. The tips of an oxygen cannula were inserted into her nostrils, held by tubes that reached behind her head. Though her complexion appeared pale, Chris was surprised to see how well she looked, especially compared to what he had mentally prepared himself for.

Rhonda was already up and walking toward him, having left the little nest she'd been settled into with Piper, Alicia, and Tommy gathered around. Roger Lemieux stood behind all of them, arms folded. Despite Roger's stoic expression, Chris imagined that he must be struggling with emotions borne of his paternal feelings for Abby. He saw deep concern in the faces of Rhonda and her children.

Rhonda put her arms around Chris, buried her face in his shoulder, and began to weep. That was more than he could bear. Though he instinctively fought back tears, his eyes were glistening, and a lump rose in his throat that threatened to turn into a sob. For a long moment, the two clung to each other, bound by their mutual love for Abby. When Chris looked over at the children, Alicia and Piper were both crying. Tommy was putting on a valiant effort to hold back tears.

"Where's Mark?" asked Chris once he and Rhonda had released one another.

"He's workin' late today. But he'll be by latah."

"How is she doing? Has there been any change?"

"No, the nurses say hah vitals ah all strong, and theyah's no internal injuries. With the way she collapsed, they wuh afraid that the pahcussion of the blast had done some internal damage. But the X-ray didn't show anything like that, and the CAT scan said she didn't suffah any nerve damage, eithah. Thank gawd. We brought in an extra chayah for you to sit in when you arrived, ovah theyah."

Roger walked over to Chris and put out his hand as if to shake it, but Chris instinctively pulled him into an awkward man-hug.

"I've got a few things to wrap up about this case," said Roger, "so I'll be heading out. Besides, we're now over the limit for the number of visitors allowed, and they've been strict about it."

"It's good to see you, Roger. At some point...."

"Yeah, I know...we can talk about what happened." Lemieux leaned in and whispered so the children wouldn't hear. "But let's give it a little time. I'm still taking it in and trying to absorb everything that went down last night. Give me a call when you're ready, and we can get together. The doctors say that they don't see any physical reason why she should be out like this right now, so they suspect psychological trauma. Let me know as soon as she comes to. In the meantime, take good care of her. Talk to her. Be with her. She'll know you're here." Then Lemieux was out the door, running nearly headlong into Andrew Coleman.

Lemieux greeted Coleman with one hand while gently closing the door with the other.

"Andrew, it's good to see you. I'm glad you're here, but you'll have to wait for someone else to leave the room before going in. They don't allow more than five visitors at a time. Chris just arrived, and Rhonda is here with her three children. Here, let's sit for a while and I'll fill you in."

Coleman and Lemieux walked over to a nearby waiting room. The two men watched the routine comings and goings of nurses, doctors, and visitors. Finally, Coleman asked, "How is Abby doing?"

"It's hard to see her like this," Lemieux replied, describing Abby's condition.

"You've known Abby for a long time," said Coleman. "Do you think she'll be able to come out of it?"

"If anyone can, she will. I've never known anyone stronger, man or woman."

"How do you mean?"

"You should have seen Abby at the Three Sisters lighthouses. It was nearly dark. She took a quick shot at one of the Artemisians from about 150 feet away, and came within inches of nailing the son of a bitch." Lemieux looked sheepishly around to see if anyone had overheard, then said under his breath, "Sorry, Andrew, I seem to be jerking back and forth between feeling grief over what happened to Abby and anger toward the crazy bastards who orchestrated this escapade. And then I feel guilty because of the awful end that they came to in the fire. There just aren't any winners here."

"Roger, you and Abby did the best you could, short of throwing yourselves into the flames."

"I appreciate that," said Lemieux, "but let's drop this line of thought and focus on Abby getting better."

"On the drive over here, I realized that Abby and I have a kind of professional friendship. I enjoy working with her a great deal, and really care about her, but it's dawning on me that I don't really know that much about her. Or about her father, for that matter—just the stories I hear at the station. You worked with Abby's father for a time, right? He sounds like a very interesting person."

Roger stared straight ahead for a time, letting his thoughts gather before speaking. "Angelo Fiorelli is one of a kind, just like his daughter. Did you know he's working at a mission in Rwanda?"

"Yes, but nothing beyond that. Abby doesn't really talk about him."

"Their relationship is good, I think, but also complicated."

"How did someone who was chief of police end up as a missionary?"

"It's a very interesting story, Andrew."

"I'm not going anywhere any time soon."

"Sure. Chief Fiorelli, Angelo, or as we sometimes called him when he was intensely pursuing a case…."

"….you mean the minister of justice."

"Exactly," Roger replied, smiling. "He attended divinity school, and was ordained as an Episcopal minister. From what he told me over the many beers we shared and during the long stakeouts we were on together, as a young man, he had been torn between encouraging people to do good in the world by continuing to serve as a minister or becoming a police officer and fighting for justice from the other end of the scale.

"My take on it was that he saw both paths as different ways of saving people's souls. So, after attending the police academy, he joined the Barnstable police force."

"It must have been kind of strange working with an officer who had baptized babies and performed weddings."

"You might think so, and at first, we were all pretty awkward around him. But he was a down to earth kind of guy; mellow and easy to be around. It didn't take long before he started to fit in at the station."

"Was he a good cop?"

"Yeah, I'll say. Angelo was a sharp investigator. His ability to focus on the details of a case that seemed to elude the rest of us—and his ability to read people well and understand their motives—produced some real breakthroughs in the cases he worked on. He also had a habit of picking up on old cases and finding leads others had missed. And then there was the infamous hit-and-run."

"What happened?"

"It was one of the most tragic cases we've ever had in Barnstable. Someone driving east on Route 6A crossed the center line and forced an oncoming car off the road, head-on into a tree. Both parents were killed instantly, but their five-year-old son was buckled up in the back seat and survived without a scratch. He was severely traumatized. No one could get him to say a word after the accident. There were no other eyewitnesses. We just kept hitting dead ends for evidence."

"What did Fiorelli do?"

Angelo knew the family well, because they used to attend his church services and they'd kept in touch. So, one day, he just showed up at the wife's sister's house, where the boy was being cared for, and asked if he could take the child out for ice cream. Somehow, in the midst of their outing, he got the boy to start talking. By the end of their time together, Angelo had learned that the other driver had stopped his car, walked over to the wreck, leaned into the driver's side window and peered into the car before driving off. And the child remembered seeing a tattoo of an anchor on the back of the man's hand. Forensics then lifted some prints off of the doorframe that matched a set of prints we had in our database for a well-known DUI repeater. When we called him in for questioning and confronted him with the information we had on the prints and the tattoo, he broke down completely and confessed."

"Did people resent Chief Fiorelli for being so good at what he did? I try to be aware of not showing anyone up when I get a breakthrough in a case."

"You might think so, but Angelo always had a way of deflecting credit onto the partners he was working with or the officers and detectives who had worked on earlier cases he had solved. Pretty unusual behavior for a cop, but something that made others appreciate his work rather than resent it. He had an easy camaraderie with coworkers."

"He sounds like a natural."

After pausing to consider what Andrew had said, Roger nodded his head. "I never thought about it in quite that way, but, yes, I'd say you're right."

"Is that why he rose up through the ranks so quickly?"

"I've often thought so. When it comes time to choose a leader, people want someone who makes them feel good about their work, and who gives them credit for what they accomplish. Angelo was that way. I don't even think he necessarily wanted the job when our old chief was retiring. But he was encouraged to apply, and floated up to the top of the applicant pool. Some people get to the top by stepping on the backs of others, and some get there by holding people up. That was Angelo. At the time, he was the youngest person ever appointed to the position."

"So, what happened? He was only chief for a few years, right?"

"My take on it? Once Angelo became chief, he realized that solving cases was what he really loved doing, not all the administrative bullshit. He hung in there for a few years, and did the department proud in terms of how he reached out to the community and built a sense of trust toward the department. But then we had a few horrific cases that I think tested his faith in people."

"Like what?"

"The worst one was a murder-suicide in a prominent family in town. No one could figure out why it had happened, and Angelo knew the family personally. It really shook him up. I remember one night, we both went out and got pretty drunk, which was not like Angelo at all. He confided in me that he had seen too much of the dark side of the human soul. A few weeks later, he resigned."

"Then what did he do?"

"He left law enforcement altogether and reentered the ministry. The next I heard, he and Abby's mother, Fiona, had left the States to work at a mission in Rwanda. That was where Abby was born."

"But they eventually came back?"

"Yes. It was heartbreaking. They returned to Barnstable when Fiona became ill and was diagnosed with cancer."

"What was it, exactly?"

"Lymphoma. They started treating her at the Mayo Clinic. When something like that happens, you find yourself learning a lot about a disease you wish you'd never had to know. Some people can live for five years or more with lymphoma, but it attacks your body's ability to fight off other diseases. In the end, after a long battle, it wasn't the cancer that took her life, but a series of complications that arose from a case of pneumonia. In a matter of days, she was gone."

"God, that must have hit Abby and her father hard."

"It broke their hearts, it really did—and those of everyone around them. Angelo was crushed. He loved Fiona, I'll tell you. And devotion? He was that rare kind of man who really thought that thinking about another woman was committing adultery in his heart—Jimmy Carter aside. He was a lucky man. Fiona was beautiful. She was kind and smart. Picture Abby with blazing red hair and a Scottish lilt."

"What happened with Abby?"

"That was the worst of all. She was always a sweet kid, and everyone loved her. What do you say to an eleven-year-old when her mother has died? I'd never felt so helpless."

"But she seems to have come out of it pretty well, after all. I mean, she's got a good heart, and she is one strong woman."

"You can say that again. After all she's been through, I don't think I've ever once heard her complain or wallow in self-pity. She directs all that energy at the perps who deserve what they get. And I'll tell you, I would not want to be on the other side of her anger."

"I've seen that fire," Coleman agreed. "When she's locked in on solving an egregious case, she's righteous."

"Oh, yeah."

"And Angelo?"

"Well, after Fiona passed away, Angelo tried returning to the ministry, but his heart just wasn't in it. Personally, I think he experienced a crisis of faith. He felt like God had abandoned him and Fiona and Abby. So, a few months after Fiona's death, he returned to police work. As it happened, the chief who had been serving at that time was stepping down, so Angelo applied."

"You mean he was appointed twice as chief?"

"Yes, believe it or not. Honestly, people had looked fondly on his previous time on the job, so he was a shoo-in. But as soon as Angelo had put in the time, he took early retirement. By then, Abby was off to college, so he returned to the mission in Rwanda, and has been working there ever since."

36

Chris walked slowly over to the chair and sat by Abby's side. He took her hand in his and gave it a light pat. "Hey, sweetie. It's me, Chris. I hope you're doing all right in there. We're all here now. Rhonda and me and all the kids: Tommy, Piper, and Alicia. And Roger was here." He began to move his fingertips lightly across the back of her hand. "You just take your time and get better. When you're ready, we'll still be here."

After some time had passed in silence, Rhonda looked up at Chris. "Can you step out faw a few minutes? Theyah ah some things I wanna tell you." Chris stood and followed Rhonda out the door, pulling it slowly shut behind him.

"So how is she, really?" he asked.

"The only real physical injury they've had tah treat is the gash in hah shouldah. The piece of glass sliced through a gap wheyah the strap on hah kevlah vest had loosened up. It went pretty deep intah the muscle tissue, deep enough that they had tah stitch inside, and then put some maw stitches on the outside. The doctah said she was lucky. Muscle tissue heals pretty fast. She also said that if the glass had hit just a little highah, it would have cut the jugulah vein at the side of hah neck, and she might have bled to death befaw the ambulance arrived."

That was when Chris realized how close he had come to losing Abby. The lump in his throat and the tears he had been trying to repress caused his words to catch. After a few minutes and several deep breaths to collect himself, he dissembled. "She's not going to like that. She prides herself on being the kind of person who is careful not to get injured on the job, or at any time, for that matter. And I don't think I've ever seen a scar anywhere...." Chris caught himself before finishing the sentence, but not soon enough.

With a devilish smile on her face, Rhonda teased, "And you wuh sayin'? Please, go on. I don't wanna miss a thing in yaw diagnosis, doctah Chris." After a brief pause during which Rhonda observed that Chris was clearly at a loss for words, she continued. "Seriously, we thought of that, too. Seeing as how young she is, the insurance company agreed to covah havin' the stitches done by a plastic surgeon. They said that the cut from the glass went deep, but that it was a clean cut, and didn't hit any tendons aw ligaments. The surgeon used tiny stitches. He came out aftah sewin' up the wound and said it would barely be visible ovah time. So, Chris...."

"What?"

"Will you keep me posted on progress with that, honey?"

For the second time since he and Rhonda had stepped out of Abigail's room, Chris had nothing.

Back inside the room, Chris could see that the children were upset and at odds after being left alone with Abigail.

Of course—she's one of the strongest women they've ever met. She's their hero, and here she is lying in a hospital bed, unconscious and looking completely helpless. The moment Chris had succeeded in turning that thought out of his mind, Rhonda leaned over Abby to kiss her forehead.

"You take cayah, sweetie," she said with glassy eyes. "We'll all come back tah visit tahmarrah. Get some rest." The children watched their mother rise. "Say goodbye tah Auntie Abby," Rhonda told them. The girls went over and kissed Abby gingerly on the forehead while Tommy stood his ground, looking like someone caught in a classic fight-or-flight struggle. Without a word, Rhonda and the children waved a silent goodbye to Chris. Just before she pulled the door closed behind her, Rhonda caught his eye and winked.

Chris sat down in the chair next to Abby. "Hi, Abby, it's me. We're alone now. I'm sorry it took me so long to get here, but I didn't hear until morning, and the rush-hour traffic out of Cambridge was barely moving. There are so many things I thought of saying to you as I was driving here, but they all seem meaningless now. You do know how dear you are to me, don't you? I have never met anyone as strong and sensitive as you. I know I spend a lot of time talking about how attractive you are to me, but I know I don't share anywhere near what I really want to say about the person I see inside, which is every bit as beautiful—even more so, if that's possible. I love you Abby, so much. You are unique and lovely, and please, dear God, come back to me."

After a long pause, he continued. "Okay, you always say

that most of what we express to one another happens at a level deeper than words, so I'm going to be quiet now and just sit here with you."

~

"Mr. Armstrong. Mr. Armstrong." Chris woke with a start and realized that someone was touching his arm. "You fell asleep, and we didn't want to wake you. Rhonda said you'd driven all the way down from Cambridge."

"What time is it?"

"It's five-fifteen, and we're just starting our morning rounds. Could you please step outside for a few minutes while I take Ms. Fiorelli's vitals and get her freshened up for the day?"

Chris was astonished to learn that he had been sleeping in that uncomfortable chair all night. His neck was extremely sore, and he tried to stretch away the pain as he waited in the corridor. After a time, the nurse emerged from the room, leaving the door ajar. She motioned that he could go back in.

"Thank you." Chris walked over to Abby's bed, yawned reflexively, and looked down to see that she had changed neither position nor expression. She lay there with the same placid countenance he'd witnessed upon arriving last evening. Chris lowered his head to hers and gently kissed her lips, holding the kiss for a long time. "Good morning, Abigail Fiorelli, little flower, love of my life." A lump filled his throat. Even if he'd had more words to say, he could not have spoken them.

When Chris reached his car, he sat down in the driver's

seat and pulled the door closed. Then he put his head in his hands and cried as if there would never be an end to the tears and the ache in his heart. It was a pain more intense than anything he'd ever felt, an agony he did not know if he had the strength to bear.

37

Rhonda reached into her purse for her mobile. "Who is it?"

"Hi, Rhonda. It's Roger, here."

"Hi, Roger. How ah yah doin'? It's good tah heah from yah. The kids ah with Mahk, and I'm heah at the hospital with Abby."

"Has there been any change? Is she responding to you at all?"

"No. She just stayahs at the ceiling. It's like she's in anothah world. But they said hah shoulder is healin' well, and theyah's no infection."

"Have you seen Chris at all?"

"Not since he came that first day to visit hah. I just don't undahstand. He's always been so steady. Fah him to just up and abandon Abby at a time like this, somethin' must have happened."

"Have you tried calling him?"

"Ovah and ovah, but all of my calls just go tah voicemail."

"But it's been nearly a week!" exclaimed Lemieux, anger creeping into his voice. "Maybe I should take a drive over to Cambridge to find him and see why the hell he hasn't come to visit."

"I knew you wuh goin' tah say that, Roger, but I don't think it's such a good idea. I have no clue what's goin' on with Chris, but theyah's a lot of strong feelin's theyah. If you and Chris got into it right now, you might drive him away."

"I'm not one for sitting around and waiting for things to happen, Rhonda. You know that."

"I totally get that, and can heah that yaw frustrated and a little pissed off," Rhonda replied. "But think about Abby. I know hah. She would only want Chris to visit if she knew he really wanted to in his haht." There was a long pause on the other end of the phone, and she could hear Roger take a couple of deep breaths.

"Okay. You and Abby are real close, so I'll trust your judgment. But when he does finally turn up, I'm going to have all I can do to keep from kicking his…."

"Roger! That's really not helping here."

"Right, I know. But if I were in Chris's shoes, I'd drop everything and be at her side 24/7."

"Roger, I don't know if you've noticed, but between the two of us, we've pretty much *been* at hah side 24/7."

"You'll let me know if you hear anything?"

"I will, honey."

"Because we need to be planning for something else before Abby comes around."

"What's that?"

"Have you seen the newspapers?"

"I saw the big story in the the *Cape Cod Times.*"

"Rhonda, the story of Abby and the Artemisians has

broken out in a big way. *The Boston Globe* picked up on the *Cape Cod Times'* lead, and then the story jumped out onto Reuters. It's in newspapers all over the world: *The Guardian, The New York Times, The Los Angeles Times*, and even *Haaretz* in the Middle East. Once the story hit social media, it went viral within hours. There are people holding vigils for Abby's recovery everywhere from the Piazza San Marco in Venice to Tiananmen Square in China and the Wailing Wall... even in front of Big Ben. Organizations like Greenpeace, the Sierra Club, and People for the Ethical Treatment of Animals are asking their members to support her. I've read that some significant donations have been coming into funds being collected for her support around the world."

"Oh....my...gawd! Abby isn't goin' tah like wakin' up tah this. She really values hah privacy, and likes tah keep things simple."

"I'm already working with the chief and the officers in Barnstable to lay a plan to keep her safe whenever she comes back to this world. But you're her closest friend, Rhonda, and she's going to need your help to get through this emotionally, especially in the first week or so."

"I'll do whatevah she needs and whatevah you ahsk, Rojah. You know that."

"I know she's a lucky person to have you as a friend."

"You sound pretty tuckahd out yawself. Go do somethin' for yawself. Cast a line in yaw fav'rite fishin' hole, aw go tah the pub and have a beah. I know Abby, and she'll come 'round when she's ready. And you know hah, too. At some level, she knows weah heah. But she doesn't like tah be pushed, eithah."

~

THE NEXT DAY, RHONDA dropped the children off at her mother's house so she could visit Abby at the hospital. It had been a whirlwind of activity since her best friend had been injured, and she wanted some quiet time to visit and think. A nurse was standing by Abby's bed checking her vital signs when Rhonda walked in.

"How is she doing?"

"Her wound is healing well, and she's stable. But there has been no change, otherwise."

When the nurse had finished updating Abby's chart and closed her laptop, Rhonda pulled a chair up next to the bed. "It's me, sweetie. How ah you doin' in theyah? I hope yaw havin' some nice dreams. Mahk and the children all asked me to say hi and tell you how much they love you, and that they miss you very much. The kids ah lovin' the book you gave them about the sea. And I'm just getting stahted on *Gift from the Sea*. I'll shut up now and do some readin', but I'm right heah, Abby." Rhonda opened the book and started to read. A few minutes later, her head lolled off to the side and she fell asleep.

~

"MOM...MOM!" FIORELLI'S HEAD BEGAN to move back and forth. Her arms were reaching out, hands opening and closing pleadingly. "MOMMY!"

Rhonda was jolted out of her sleep by the commotion.

When she realized what was happening, she reached out to take her friend's hands and tried to calm her down. She could see that Abby's breathing was quick, erratic, and shallow. Alarms were screaming from the monitors.

"Abby, it's me, Rhonda. Yaw okay, sweetie. Yaw doing fine."

Fiorelli's eyes darted back and forth for a time as she tried to understand where she was. When she turned her head to look at Rhonda, her eyes settled there, and she recognized her friend's loving, familiar face.

"Rhonda? What's going on?"

Rhonda's tears of joy could not be stopped. She held onto Abby's hands. "You've been gone faw a little while, honey, but now yaw back. Yaw in the hospital, and everythin's all right."

Fiorelli's eyes swept around the hospital room. She was still getting her bearings. "How long have I been here, Rhon?"

"For about a week, dear. The doctors and nurses have been takin' good care of you."

Abby reached up to touch Rhonda's face, then winced at the sharp pain in her shoulder.

"You just rest, Abby. You had a bad cut in your shouldah, and some stitches. It's healin' well, but it's goin' tah hurt for anothah week aw two." Rhonda gathered herself up before asking the next question. "Now, I know this is goin' tah seem like a strange question…but…wheyah have yah been?" Tears welled from Fiorelli's eyes and streamed down her face. "I'm so sorry I asked. Was it horrible?"

"No, Rhon. I'm only crying because I can't remember

the last time I was so happy. I've been with my mother, and it was wonderful. I was a little girl again...."

The two friends sat holding hands as Abby told of her excursions with her mother, recalling their conversations and retracing precisely the sights, sounds, and smells of the childhood she had relived over the past week. The sun arced over the top of the sky. Nurses came and went to make periodic checks on Abby's vital signs, but for Abby and Rhonda, they were truly the only two people in existence. In those magical hours, Rhonda sat, listened, and was swept up in the realm of her friend's childhood. She could not recall a time in her life when she had ever felt this close to another human being. Just before she left to go home, Rhonda took her friend's hand. In a serious tone, she said, "Abby, theyah's somethin' I have tah tell yah befaw I go."

"Is everybody okay?" Fiorelli asked, an urgent tone tingeing her voice.

"No, honey, it's nothin' like that."

"Then what, Rhon?"

"Well, while you've been recovahing, the story kind of grew."

"Did they cover it in the *Globe*?"

"Not exactly."

"Rhon, then what?!"

"Okay. Calm down. It's not quite like when Princess Di was in that cah accident, but it's not fah off."

"What?!"

"People all ovah the wuhld is prayin' fah ya, hopin' fah

news that yaw gettin' bettah. I'm only sayin' so yah cahn prepayah yawself." Rhonda looked at the expression in her friend's face, and it was just as she had feared: a deer caught in the headlights. "It's just that people want tah show they cayah. When some children in Rwanda found out that you grew up in theyah country, they recawded a blessing song and posted it on YouTube. It's wondahful."

The two women hugged for a long time. Finally, Rhonda picked up her purse, but by the time she had reached the door, Fiorelli's quick mind had not only started to take in the news, but was beginning to prepare for what was to come.

38

Chris awoke to the same hollow feeling he'd been wrestling with ever since he'd visited Abby in the hospital. Since the long drive back to Cambridge that morning, he'd slid into a state of inner numbness. His senses felt dull. It was as if he were viewing the world through a layer of gauze separating him from the people and pleasures in which he usually reveled. Chris had heard the expression *going through the motions* many times before, but he'd never known what it really felt like until now.

Again, this morning, Chris couldn't be bothered to shave, so he walked into the kitchen and turned on the coffeemaker. Then he shuffled over to the front door of his apartment, opened it, and stooped to pick up the daily copy of *The Boston Globe*.

Sitting down at the kitchen table, he took a sip of his coffee and opened the newspaper to discover the story right on the bottom of Page One: "Barnstable Detective Remains in Coma Following Raid on Mysterious Cult."

"Damn it!" he cursed out loud. "She's not in a coma!" Then he couldn't think of how to describe the state of existence in which Abby found herself. *Can emotional trauma be considered a coma?* As he sat and pondered this crucial question, Chris glanced over at the stack of ungraded exams from the round of summer classes that had just ended. Only one thought came to mind, and those five words described precisely how he felt about his life in this state of limbo. They had been echoing around inside his head like a mantra ever since he'd seen Abby lying in that hospital bed: *I really don't care anymore.*

Some time later, Chris realized he'd been staring at the same paragraph in the newspaper for a long while. He couldn't even concentrate enough to read an entire news story. For the past week, he hadn't been able to focus on his work, the book he was reading, or even his favorite nature shows on PBS. *Where the hell is my mind?* When he'd finished his coffee and gone to place the empty cup in the sink, all Chris could think was, *where did all these dirty dishes come from?*

I've got to get out of here. Throwing on some clothes, Chris grabbed a hat, binoculars, and the key to his apartment, and soon found himself walking west along Brattle Street toward the Mount Auburn Cemetery, past all the familiar landmarks. As he walked by the Longfellow House, he recalled how Abby had seen hints of Etruscan patterning in the arrangement of slats on the elaborate wooden fence out front. Arriving at Trinity Church, he looked up at the arches over the windows and doors, and the high, curving vault that surrounded it all. Chris remembered how excited Abby had been to recognize the elements of Richardsonian Romanesque architecture in the design—and the way she'd continued on about the fact that the formal style was found on many public libraries built by wealthy benefactors during the nineteenth century throughout New England. He remembered thinking, *I have never met anyone who knew so much about so many things, and in such depth. And that wonderful mind is now off in some other place, and may not ever come back to me again.*

Finally, Chris crossed the road and found himself looking up at the larger-than-life inscription on the granite archway at the cemetery entrance. On their first visit there together, Abby had looked up and exclaimed, "Did you know that this is a rare example of Egyptian Revival? This archway was the first of its kind in the United States when it was built in 1842. It looks like a design borrowed from Tutankhamun's tomb!" On this day, however, Chris stopped to read the inscription from Ecclesiastes 12:7, which again reminded him of Abby, the only person he knew who had actually committed the Bible to memory and could somehow pull a quote from scripture out of the blue to perfectly suit any given situation.

THEN SHALL THE DUST RETURN
TO THE EARTH AS IT WAS
AND THE SPIRIT SHALL RETURN
UNTO GOD WHO GAVE IT.

Soon after entering beneath the archway, Chris wandered along the pathways that bordered the dense shrubs growing along the marshy edge of Halcyon Lake. He examined one particular place where, on the first springtime birding walk he had ever taken with Abby at Auburn Cemetery, they had both gotten a spectacular look at a rare cerulean warbler near the Mary Baker Eddy Monument, its jewel-like azure shimmering in the clear vernal light. It was the first time either of them had ever seen that particular species, and the fact that they'd seen it together struck Chris as a good omen. In many ways, he knew he'd fallen in love with Abby from the first time they'd met. If he could pinpoint one moment of realization that the roots of nascent love had grown deep in his heart, it was sharing the sighting of that bejeweled warbler with her.

Chris continued to wander the maze of trails, passing the Bigelow Sphinx, numerous lions, and several angels, some of which were so beautiful and lifelike, they made his heart catch. The experience evoked a desire to speak with the angels about the theological questions with which he always struggled. At last, he found himself standing in front of the statue of Hygieia, whom Abby had said was the Greek Goddess of Health and Hygiene, daughter of Asclepius, God of Medicine. At that moment, Chris's mind surged toward the purple milkweed, *Asclepias purpurascens*, that Abby had asked him to verify during her research on the Artemisians. With that thought, he became aware of the futility of trying to escape the pain he knew, at some level, he was running from.

The realization overcame his defenses and caused tears to flow freely. Chris sobbed convulsively until his nose ran and his eyes reddened. Time and again, grief broke upon his heart like waves crashing on the shore. Through a veil of tears, he gazed at the blurry image of Hygieia. *Heal this, if you can. How can I spend the rest of my life watching her walk out the door every day and wondering if she's ever going to come home?*

39

Fiorelli's exit from the hospital had the feeling of a home-coming parade. Rhonda, Mark, and the children followed the attendant wheeling Abby along the hallway toward the front lobby. Andrew Coleman and Chief Morales were waiting at the portico to greet her. Roger stood by his car with the front passenger door open. Everyone important in Abby's life was present to see her out of the hospital and on her way home. Everyone, that is, but Chris.

The story of the Artemisians had continued to garner significant attention and sympathy for Fiorelli worldwide. For nearly a week, countless souls had been holding their breath, waiting to find out if the tenacious detective Abigail Fiorelli would emerge from her state of unconsciousness and return to the world of the living.

Fortunately, the Barnstable Police Department had anticipated the crush of reporters and well-wishers, and had cordoned off a clear space so Fiorelli's wheelchair could make it from the front door of the hospital to Lemieux's awaiting car.

Still, the intensity of the noise and commotion caught Fiorelli off guard, and it was almost more than she could bear. She couldn't wait to speed off in the direction of the peace and quiet at her cottage by Sandy Neck Beach.

Just before she got into the car, however, Abby suddenly felt compelled to address the crowd. "Roger, please stop here for a minute. I just want to say something to thank all of these people." Someone offered a wireless microphone, and Lemieux handed it over to Fiorelli. As soon as everyone saw that she was about to speak, the crowd settled down. Everyone became so quiet that Abby could actually hear the wind blowing through the leaves of the scarlet oak branches arching overhead.

"I want to thank all of you for your prayers and good wishes. From the bottom of my heart, I am grateful to everyone involved in solving this case, and to my friends and family, who offered their support this past week. We did everything we could to put a stop to these heinous crimes against innocent endangered animals. We wanted no one to be hurt, and we deeply regret that the case ended so tragically. Our prayers go out to all who lost their lives as well as their families. Godspeed."

Once in the car, Roger and Abby sat in silence for a time, absorbing and appreciating her sudden return to consciousness and the drama of the media crush. After some time had passed, Lemieux remarked, "Fiorelli, I really admire how you pulled yourself together in such a short time and made such an eloquent speech off the cuff."

"I couldn't just get into the car without thanking all of those people."

"Yes, you could have, but that would not have been your way. People from all around the world have been holding vigils, waiting and praying for you to heal and awaken from wherever your mind has been. There has been so much love coming to you in your absence—you can't imagine. Like it or not, you're no longer an anonymous detective from Barnstable. You're a heroine to millions of people who care deeply about the well-being of endangered animals and what we're doing to the planet."

"What do you think this will mean for my everyday life?"

"Only time will tell, but one thing's for certain: You'll have the opportunity to make an impact with your life's work, way beyond anything you could ever have imagined." The pair sat in silence as Fiorelli tried to absorb the enormity of what Roger had just conveyed. "Now that you're back in the world of mere mortals, is there anything you'd like me to get for you on the way home?"

"Actually, Roger, there is."

"What's that? You name it, Abby."

"I'd like to stop off and get a cone of Amaretto Cherry Chip ice cream at Smitty's. That would really hit the spot. I don't know what they've been putting down my throat during the past week, but it feels like it was the size of a small tree and with really rough bark. Something cool and sweet would be a good step toward putting this unbelievable experience behind me."

"Now you're talking!"

"What's *your* favorite?"

"All ice cream tastes good to me, but at Smitty's, I'm partial to Shark's Tooth."

"Jeez, Roger, what's the point of eating a nice ice cream cone if it's only going to bite back?"

Lemieux smiled, but didn't respond to Fiorelli's joke. No ice cream cone would ever be as sweet as hearing Abby's quick retort and letting it linger in the air. It proved for certain that she was, indeed, back. For the moment, all felt right in the world.

As Lemieux walked back to the car carrying the two heaping ice cream cones, he had to lick the drippings off the melting scoops of Shark's Tooth. Approaching the passenger-side door, he handed Fiorelli her Amaretto Cherry Chip along with a few napkins before going around and getting in on the driver's side. The two sat wordlessly for a time, occasional groans of satisfaction accentuating their favorite flavors. Then, without any forewarning, Fiorelli burst out, "Roger? I have a personal question."

Lemieux hung his cone out the window to keep it from dripping on the upholstery. "What is it, Abby?"

"Where is Chris?"

It took Lemieux so long to respond that Fiorelli began to wonder if he had heard her question. He remembered Rhonda's admonition that coming down too hard on Chris might alienate Abby from someone she cared deeply about. When he did speak, his tone was controlled and measured.

"Chris was by your side right away when you were admitted to the hospital. The nurses allowed him to spend that first night sleeping in the chair next to you. When we didn't see him for a few days, we asked the nurses if he'd been in. The one who'd been on duty the morning he left said he looked pretty shaken up. Someone saw him breaking up as he sat in his car before driving back to Cambridge."

"But didn't he know I was being discharged today?"

"No, I don't think he did. We haven't been able to reach him all week, so I don't think he knew."

Lemieux cast a discreet sideways glance at Fiorelli. He could see the hurt in her face. Not wanting to say anything else to heighten those feelings, he sat and waited in silence until it was clear that she had accepted what he'd shared and wasn't inclined to press him further. They finished their ice cream cones in silence, but the moment had lost some of its luster.

~

WHEN LEMIEUX TURNED THE car into Fiorelli's gravel driveway, she noticed two patrol cars flanking the end of the lane. Several officers were conversing with a media van along the shoulder of the road.

Lemieux caught the quizzical look on Abby's face. "Nothing to be concerned about. The patrols are just precautionary. There haven't been any threats or anything like that, but as I said, there's been a lot of press about this case and your role in solving it. We just want to protect your privacy while you're recovering."

"I wasn't totally surprised," Abby replied. "That kind of thing is protocol. I'm just not used to being the subject offered protection. You know…being on that side of the action. I'll sleep better, though, knowing they've got my back. Please tell everyone at the station that I really appreciate everything they've done." Fiorelli waved at the officers as they drove by.

"Are you sure you're going to be okay tonight?" asked Lemieux, grabbing her overnight case from the trunk and carrying it toward the cottage. "Rhonda said she'd be happy to come and keep you company. And I'd be glad to stay for a while, if you'd like."

"I think I'll be fine, Roger. Thank you for offering. The quiet is going to be a blessing, to be honest. I've hardly slept in the last 24 hours, and I suspect that being unconscious for a week isn't exactly conducive to maintaining routine sleep rhythms."

Sometimes, when Abby made comments like that, Lemieux wasn't sure if she was being straight up or if it was another one of her dry cerebral jokes. Whenever he was uncertain, he tried not to laugh, figuring she would be less offended if she thought he didn't get the joke. He didn't want to laugh at something that wasn't intended to be funny. Besides, it was part of a larger issue he was aware of on the force: Men and women often had very different notions of what was funny and what wasn't. When they reached the door, Lemieux brought the overnight case just inside the threshold and put it down.

Fiorelli thought he was acting rather sheepish. "Thank you so much for bringing me home, Roger. And for the ice cream! I can't tell you how much it means to me that you and

Rhonda were by my side while I was in the hospital. I will always remember that kindness. Would you like to come in for something to drink before going home?"

"I'd like to, I really would. And I don't know if my age is showing or not, but I'm suddenly feeling pretty tired myself. It's probably better if I just head home at this point, but let's get together soon for a drink. When you're ready, I can answer any questions you might have about the aftermath of the case."

"Sounds like a good plan," Abby replied, walking over to Roger and giving him a warm hug.

"You take good care, Fiorelli. Go easy on yourself. You've been through an awful lot in the past week."

"You, too, Roger. And stay alert on the drive home."

Lemieux turned quickly toward the door so that Fiorelli wouldn't see the tears he could no longer hold back. He'd had to rein them in ever since she had collapsed in his arms following the explosion.

40

Fiorelli walked into the bathroom and looked in the mirror. She didn't know if it was the painkiller the hospital had been giving her or fatigue from the ordeal itself, but she had never looked so tired. Still, she was craving a bath and a cup of hot chamomile tea. She drew a bath and put on the teakettle.

Abby loved the bathroom in her cottage. The house had been built in the 1930s, and still had the traditional claw foot tub and marble-top sink from the era. The walls were faced up to the chair rail with varnished wainscoting, and the floor was covered in linoleum: a basket-weave pattern with a border of flowers. The windows featured the old wavy glass that projected no end of fascinating patterns of sunlight and moonlight onto the irregular surfaces of the plaster walls. Looking out into the darkness that had now settled in, Abby drew down the shade, undressed, and put on a robe.

Just as she was turning off the faucets in the tub, the teakettle started to sing. Fiorelli poured her tea, placed it on a small stand next to the tub, and slowly eased into the slightly-too-hot water, groaning with delight as her entire being seemed to melt and relax. The humidity rising from the water brought out the odd smell that sometimes came from the wainscoting next to the tub—a combination of old yellow pine and varnish, she figured. It wasn't necessarily a pleasant scent, but it was as familiar as an old shoe, and so comforting. She remembered to sit upright in the tub so as not to wet the wound dressing on her shoulder.

After what seemed like just a few minutes, Fiorelli found her head jerking up from sleep. Alarmed that she might drop off again and slide into the tub, she stood up carefully, putting most of her weight into her uninjured left shoulder and drying off as best she could with one arm. Abby put on the nightclothes she'd draped over the towel rack, picked up her nearly-full cup of tea, and walked toward the bedroom.

Placing her cup on the nightstand, Abby opened the chest at the end of her bed. Inside was a floral stationery box containing letters from her father and mother.

There was nothing in life Abby valued more than the series of letters her mother had written to her in the years before she died, even as the cancer had slowly stolen her away from family and the beauty of the natural world she loved so dearly. When Fiona first realized that she might not be present to teach her little girl—or share her life with the adolescent and grown woman Abigail would become—she had begun writing a series of letters for Abby to read at different stages of her life. In them, Fiona shared what she considered the most salient life lessons for Abby to learn as she grew up.

Fiorelli had read each letter so many times, the corners

had become somewhat grayed, and the paper was now darkly faded from exposure over the passing years. Having just spent so much time with her mother in another realm, Abby felt an intense sense of anticipation about reading one letter in particular tonight.

At some point in her early twenties, Abby had begun referring to her mother as Fiona, just as she might have done had her mother survived. Over the past week, visiting with her mother in her mind's eye, Abby had sensed her own age to be five, well before her mother's death. So, on this night, she pulled out the first letter her mother had written to her as a young girl. Anticipating how she would feel, Abby placed a box of tissues on the bedspread, gently unfolded the letter, and read.

To My Sweet Abigail:

If you are reading this letter, Abigail, then I will have already gone on to see God. I will not tell you not to cry, or not to be sad, because those are the things we do when someone we love goes away. It is okay, sweetie, to cry whenever you need to. Crying is our heart's way of letting us know how much we love one another. When you miss someone you care for, your tears are your love pouring out into the world. Don't ever be ashamed to cry, and to show others how much your heart is able to love.

You are so dear to me—dearer than anyone in the world. Please believe that I would never have left you if I'd had a choice. When someone gets sick and goes away, it is not because they don't love the people they leave behind. It is because the way

*of the world is for every living thing to live out its life as fully
as possible, but to then accept that everyone reaches a place when
they have had their turn and their life is complete. I would have
given anything for my turn to have been longer so I could have
spent many, many more years with you and your father. But that
was not God's plan for my life.*

*Most of all, my dear, sweet girl, don't ever, ever think that
my dying was your fault in any way. Sometimes, when we lose
someone we love, our mind plays tricks on us. Our thoughts sometimes make us wonder: If only we had done something differently,
or had not done something at all, maybe that person would still
be alive. No, baby…that is not true. Nothing you have ever done
had anything to do with the fact that I died. In truth, the love
you shared with me and the light you brought into my life every
day kept me in this world far longer.*

*I once told you that Abigail means joy of the father, but you
brought great joy to me, too; and you will always bring joy to
everyone who comes to truly know what a kind and caring heart
you have to share. I am so proud of you.*

*You will always be in my heart, and I will always be in your
heart. I will speak to you again in my letters as you grow up.
Please don't think of them as my way of saying goodbye. In fact,
they are my way of continuing to say hello.*

*If there is anything in this letter you don't understand, please
do not worry. You can read my letters at any age, and they will
speak to you in different ways because you will be ready to hear
and understand more as you grow older and become wiser yourself.*

*Whenever you want to speak with me, just think or say out
loud whatever you want to share. I am here in Heaven with a*

forever of time to wait and listen for your sweet voice to reach me. I love you, darling, and I always will.

> *Your loving mother,*
> *Fiona*

After Abby had finished the letter and was dabbing away tears, she marveled at how such a sad—and, on its face, tragic—letter could offer comfort in this moment of turmoil. She often thought the greatest wisdom Fiona had passed down was this: The most important thing is to live in a way that's true to yourself in everything you say, do, and think.

Everything I did that affected the events of the past few weeks...was it all true to myself and what I believe? The answer came back to Abby clearly, with no hesitation. *Yes. As tragically as things turned out, you followed a clear path, seeking justice that led to a moment of truth. You did all you could to save those souls. The rest was out of your hands.*

Abby also knew that it would take a very long time for her heart to hear what her mind was trying to say. Her soul would have to walk through a time of darkness and pain before light would restore her life to the way it had been before she had been touched by the evil of the Artemisians.

41

Chris was jolted out of a fitful sleep by the ringtone on his cell phone. He rolled over and picked up the receiver. "Hello?"

"Hi, Chris, there you are," said his good friend Noah. "Where have you been? I've been calling all morning."

"Hey, Noah. What's up?"

"We're getting together for lunch, that's what's up. Clean yourself up and meet me at Toscano's at noon."

A short time later, Noah walked through the front door of the restaurant. The waitress pointed to the table where Chris was already seated. To Noah's surprise, an attractive coed had been sitting with Chris, and was just getting up from her chair. Before she left, both she and Chris laughed at something. Noah watched her reach out and put her hand on Chris's shoulder. He passed her as he approached the table, turning to watch her walk out the door before sitting down across from Chris.

"Hey, Noah."

"Hi, Chris. Say, I've been meaning to ask you a question."

"What's that?"

"The other day, you said you appreciate that I'm the kind of person who tells it like it is, remember?"

"Yes, I remember," Chris replied, his guard going up.

"So, let me ask you a question."

"Okay."

"What the hell are you doing?"

Chris was taken aback by his friend's bluntness. "What are you talking about?"

"What's with the casual tête-à-tête with Amanda? Since when did the two of you start getting together outside of class? Isn't she one of your graduate teaching assistants?"

"What of it?" asked Chris defensively. "I got here early and she was just finishing her meal, so I decided to join her for a drink while I was waiting for you."

"That didn't look like a casual meeting to me. Have you two been seeing each other?"

"What's with the interrogation?"

"You're avoiding my question."

"Just casually. We're just…you know…friends."

"Now that's a line I never thought I'd hear coming from you. Let me ask you another question."

"Go for it, Noah. Why hold back now?" As soon as the words were out of his mouth, Chris regretted the sarcasm in his own voice.

"How's Abigail doing? And, while we're at it, when was the last time you drove down to Barnstable to see her?" Once Noah saw the crestfallen expression on Chris's face, he softened to his friend's plight and attempted to take the conversation to a better place. "Look, I didn't mean to be so confrontational. Really, I'm concerned about you—holed up in your apartment, missing classes. Everyone in the biology department is worried. Some of your colleagues reached out to me because they know we're friends. They've been following the story in the newspapers, and they're worried about how it's impacting you."

"You should have seen her in that hospital bed, Noah. She's the strongest person I know, and there she was, helpless. Until that moment, I hadn't realized how much I relied on her strength. It dawned on me that for the first time in my entire life, I'd come to need another person, and it shook me to the core."

"It sounds to me like you're afraid, and that fear is ruling your life."

"What if Abby and I stay together? How can I endure the uncertainty and pain of constantly fearing that she will simply go to work one day and never come home?"

"So you thought you'd take fate into your own hands and make your future more certain by leaving her?"

"I'm not...."

"Sure, you are. And I have to be honest; it's the cowardly way out. You're afraid of losing someone you love, but instead of facing that fear, you're distancing yourself. You are at risk of doing something stupid that will mean you can never go back to what you've had with Abby. So ask yourself: Is it more important to avoid the pain you *imagine* could come in the future, or to live each day and cherish every minute while you have Abigail in your life now? If something ever happened to her, sure, you'd feel the pain. But it wouldn't be anything like the regret and remorse you're going to feel if you spend the rest of your life trying to live with the fact that it was your choice to throw your chance at happiness away."

The truth in his friend's words came crashing down on Chris's world, shattering what he thought had already broken. Then a new and more urgent fear began to rise in his heart: that of losing Abby's trust, and her love, forever.

"And by the way, don't forget that I've met Abigail," Noah continued. "And let me tell you something, in case you haven't thought about this, either. Once you've danced with the gods, you will never, ever again find happiness with mere mortals."

As Chris stared at his friend, the proverbial scales fell from his eyes. "Oh, my God, Noah. What a fool I've been."

"No argument there, my friend. Now, there's only one existential question you need to ask yourself at this critical, defining juncture of your life."

"What's that?"

"Just how fast can a 1960 Corvette get from Cambridge to Cape Cod?"

"Thank you, Noah," blurted Chris, standing up so quickly that he almost knocked over his chair. "You're a real godsend."

"I doubt that. But a prophet...maybe."

∽

As soon as Chris had settled into the driver's seat, he pulled out his mobile and dialed Rhonda's number. He found himself shaken by the news Rhonda shared as they spoke, and began to deeply regret his absence. He couldn't believe he'd missed all the time he could have been by Abby's side, and that she'd already come home from the hospital.

"Wheyah have yah been, Chris, when she needed yah maw than evah? We've been callin' and emailin' and textin' yah faw days, but no one's huhd a thing. What's goin' on? Ah yah awright? We stahted tah get worried."

Chris sat and listened as Rhonda continued to speak, but was so ashamed that he couldn't think of much to say. After a while, not wanting to delay his trip any more than necessary, he said goodbye as politely as he could, rang off, and started the engine. He drove off, glancing furtively between his odometer and the speed limit signs, watching the time like a hawk.

42

On the drive to Barnstable, Chris kept playing pieces of the conversation with Rhonda over in his head.

"She has holed hahself up in the cottage, and refuses to see anyone or ansah hah phone. I've tried to visit, and so has Rojah, but she won't even ansah the daw. I've never seen hah like this, Chris. I don't think she's hahself. She's one strong woman, but I don't think anyone could experience what she went through without serious repahcussions. I feayah for hah. She needs you, Chris."

"But why didn't she call me? I would have been there in a heartbeat."

"She knows that yah came to see hah when she first went into the hospital, and that yah stayed that night. But she also knows that yah haven't been back again since. She was deeply hurt that yah wuhn't theyah when she woke up and left the hospital. She doesn't know what's goin' on with yah, and she's feelin' vulnerable."

"I'm on my way."

"Drive safe, Chris. And please call me as soon as yah have some news about Abby. Me and the children ah so worried about hah."

It seemed like an eternity before Chris finally heard the familiar crunch of gravel as he turned into the drive to Abby's cottage. He cut the engine, gathered himself, walked up to the door, and gently knocked.

"Abby...it's me, Chris." He waited for a response. "Sweetheart, I want to see you and help you get through this. Please open the door." Still, there was no sound. "I'm so sorry I didn't come to see you this week. It hurt so much to see you suffering, and I've been weak. But I'm here now. Please open the door so I can explain and try to make it up to you. Please, honey." Several minutes passed in silence.

Chris was about to knock again when he heard some muffled sounds inside the house. He waited to see what would happen before pressing further. The sound of shuffling feet approached, the latch clicked, and the door slowly swung open. Fiorelli stood before him, a ghost of her usual self. She looked tired, wan, and unkempt, as if she hadn't bathed or eaten since arriving home.

Without making eye contact, Abby looked down, turned, and shuffled back toward the bedroom. Her movements were mechanical. Chris followed without saying a word.

Fiorelli sat down on the bed and stared out the window, glassy-eyed. Chris saw no expression on her face whatsoever. She looked as if the life force had been drained out of her, leaving a pale void in its place. He waited for a time to see if she would say anything. "Abby," he implored. "Tell me how I can help you."

"I don't know if anyone really can," she finally replied. "How do you go on living a normal life after experiencing the things I saw? Those flames, the screams, and worst of all, the smell? I can't get it out of my head. It makes the normal, everyday things seem like they're no longer important or meaningful. How *can* they be, if something like that is possible in the world?"

"But you've seen all kinds of criminal behavior in your career. Why is this so different?"

"If there's a line between bad and evil, what the Artemisians were doing crossed that line. And witnessing that kind of evil firsthand has left a stain on my soul that I can't get out."

"That stain will fade with time, Abby. You've been through horrible experiences, and you've seen evil in this job before, but you've always been able to move on after some time has passed. I can take some time off to be with you, if you like."

"But that's not all."

Chris took her hands and tried to look into her eyes. "What else? Please tell me."

Abby began to sob uncontrollably, pulling tissues from the box on her nightstand and blowing her nose. "No one deserves to die like that, Chris. It was horrible. We tried to get inside to pull them out, but once the door was blocked, we couldn't reach them. Even if we had been able to, the flames spread so fast, and the heat...."

"Abby, look at me, please."

Fiorelli wiped the tears from her face and neck, then blew her nose again. Still, she would not look at him.

"Abby, this was not your fault. You do know that, right? You did everything you could, short of throwing yourself into the flames. Look at your hands."

Chris could see clearly that the fine hairs had been burned away and her skin was still red. She had bandages on both hands where small blisters had formed. Puss was beginning to seep through the bandages.

"I don't want to talk about it anymore, Chris."

"Okay. Not talking is fine."

"Would you do something for me?"

"Anything, Abby."

"Just hold me."

"Okay, but first we have to change your bandages." Chris went into the bathroom, opened the medicine cabinet, and took out a roll of wound dressing, some antibiotic ointment, and a box of sterile gauze pads. He ran the water until it was warm and moistened one of the pads. Taking one hand at a time, he gently pulled back the dressings. Once the raw skin was exposed, he dabbed at it gently, knowing full well from his own prior experience just how much it was going to hurt. Abby didn't even flinch. It was as if her entire body had gone numb, not just her emotions.

Once her wounds had been re-bandaged, Chris cradled Abby's hands in his upturned palms and looked at her face. For the first time since his arrival, she made eye contact. He struggled to keep his face unreactive when he saw the hollowness in those usually warm, caring, joyful eyes. "Honey. Why don't you lie down here next to me?" Chris lay on his side, patting the mattress in front of him.

Abby turned her back to Chris and lay down, legs pulled up in front of her. He moved in close, reaching out and gently stroking her head. In all the time they had been together, he had never seen her so vulnerable. His emotions were a mix of tenderness and concern at seeing someone so strong in such an unguarded state of despair. "Abby, your hands and shoulder will heal just fine, but you're still in emotional shock, and that is going to take time to heal. I'm so sorry it hurts so much right now."

The two of them lay that way for a long time as Chris continued to comb his fingers through her hair. The mellifluous notes of a song sparrow drifted through the window, wafting inside with the sweet scent of the jasmine growing in a pot on the patio. He noticed that the shadow pattern cast by the sun through the windowpanes had moved far from where it had been when they first lay down. Chris felt Abby's breathing settle into a slow, steady rhythm, and knew that she had, at last, fallen asleep.

43

Chris awakened, laying with his eyes closed for a few moments before remembering that he was in Abby's bed. Gradually, the events of the previous night filtered into his mind. He often wished that the brief, dreamy moments of bliss after sleep could linger before the reality of each morning rushed in upon him, but today, it was not to be. Just as he opened his eyes, an owl called from a stand of pitch pines outside the open window with a series of deep notes sung at long intervals: *hoo…hoo…hoo…hoo…hoo…hoo…hoo….* He recognized it as the voice of a long-eared owl, a species rarely encountered on Cape Cod. *My birding friends aren't going to believe this unless I record it.* He took out his phone, called up the memo app, and held the phone up toward the open window. Silence.

Disappointed, Chris looked over to his right at an empty bed. He reached out and felt a hollow in the blanket where Abby should have been sleeping. He looked around the room, but she was gone. "Abby?" he called, but there was no answer. Rolling to the edge of the mattress and sitting up, Chris reached down and put on his shoes, recalling the last time he had slept with clothes on at the hospital. "Abby?" he called again, walking into the kitchen, only to be met with silence. The coffee maker was cold, and the dirty dishes in the sink were just as they had been when he'd arrived last night. Abigail was gone.

Chris went into the bathroom and brushed his teeth to get rid of the cottony feeling in his mouth. He walked to the front door, grabbed the key from its hook, and locked the door behind him. Following his instincts, he walked up the driveway, took a right on Sandy Neck Road, and headed down to the trailhead. It had rained in the early hours before sunrise, and a ghostly mist was lingering in the hollows behind the dunes. A soft sea breeze washed over him, its pleasant warmth a harbinger of the intense heat that would rise later in the day as the rays of sun seared into the soft sand.

It had been hot and dry for several days, and Chris reveled in one of his favorite aromas as the sharp tang of petrichor wafted up from the earth, a distinct ozone-like scent emanating from the ground after the rain. He had read that the smell came from a compound called *geosmin* produced by soil bacteria. To his nose, the unique scent fell somewhere between pleasant and pungent, reminding him that life presented an endless stream of contradictory senses and emotions, and that we all yield to unbidden sensations of pain and pleasure, just as a reed bends in the wind. *How can the love I feel for Abigail make me so happy one moment, but in the next, cause my heart to feel unbearable pain at the thought of losing her?*

When Chris reached the gatehouse, he turned right,

following the nature trail that skirted the boundary between dune and marsh. He strongly suspected that Abby might have walked in the direction of a short spur that cut toward a certain small, shallow pool. She loved to go there and sit for hours as the world of birds and wind and sky cycled around her.

After walking for ten minutes or so, following what he thought were Abby's tracks in the sand, Chris was about to turn down the trail when he happened to glance up toward the top of the dune. Abigail was there, facing out into a strong ocean breeze that caused her hair and the shawl wrapped around her shoulders to whip and billow. His heart leapt at the vision of her auburn locks burnished by the faint blush of dayspring. She was at one with the elements, the land and the sea. To Chris's eyes, Abigail was no less than a goddess: Aurora calling in the dawn.

Feet working through the yielding sands as he climbed the face of the dune, Chris arrived at Abby's side. She continued to stare out into the wind. He sensed that she was aware of his presence, but she did not turn to face him. For a long time, they stood next to each other as the pastel hues on the horizon slowly brightened into early morning light. Gulls wheeled overhead. Sanderlings poked the sands stretched before them with probing beaks, dancing with the incoming waves, marking with each turn-and-run the same rhythms of the seashore that have heralded daybreak since time out of mind.

"My mother used to tell me the story," Abby began, "of

a small farm, a croft up in the highlands of Scotland on the Isle of Rùm. The husband and wife who lived there had some sheep and cattle, but their three sons were getting older, and the land would soon be unable to provide for them."

"So what did they do?" Chris asked, immediately regretting that he'd interrupted her. He waited for her to resume her story, which she did in the lilting dialect she had picked up from her relations in Scotland. Chris loved to hear this warm, pleasant accent, which Abigail rarely used.

"The father, who was devout, put down the Bible he was reading one night and called his three sons to his side, saying to the oldest boy, 'Hamish, you're getting to be of the marryin' age, but our wee croft is nee big enough tah support another family.'

And his son replied, 'But Dah, what am I goin' tah do?'

'Well,' said his father, 'As yee know, I used to be a fisherman. I still have me boat, and I could teach you the trade. Put your mind to it, and you could support a family of your own.'

'Aye, Dah, that would be grand!' exclaimed Hamish.

'But whatever yee do, Hamish, duh nee ever go fishin' out by Seal Island. Them waters and those fish are meant for the seal folk alone.'

'Yes, Dah.'

'Does yah hear me, Hamish?'

'Aye, Dah, aye. There'll be nee fishin' out by Seal Island.'

'Well, all right, then.'

Each day, Hamish's father took him out in the boat and taught him how to be a fisherman: how to cast the nets and haul in the catch, how to bring the fish to market and barter for a good price.

One day, while Hamish was at market selling his fish, he saw another young fisherman who always seemed to catch more fish than anyone else.

'How do yah do it?' asked Hamish. 'Yah always have the biggest catch.'

'Oh, aye,' said the young fisherman, leaning in to tell Hamish his secret. 'Take yer boat out to Seal Island. There's more fish in them there waters than yee can imagine!'

The very next morning, Hamish sailed out to Seal Island. As soon as he cast his net into the water, it filled with fish, but many were half-eaten by the seals before he could bring the net into the boat. And the seals had chewed great holes in his net. It was the same every time Hamish fished out by Seal Island.

'Bloody seals,' he said. 'They're eating half the fish and destroying me nets!'

One night after supper, Hamish told his father, 'Dah, we're going down to the boat to mend the nets.'

'Alright, then, boys,' his father replied, 'but be careful. There could be a storm blowin' in from the north.'

'Aye, Dah, we'll be careful.'

When Hamish and his brothers got to the boat, Hamish told them, 'We're goin' out tah Seal Island. We're goin' tah catch them seals when they haul out onto the rocks at the end of the day. Then we'll club them tah death and have all the fish to ourselves.'

'No, Hamish, no!' his little brother said. 'Dah said tah leave them Seal Folk alone.'

'Duh nee worry, Gareth. It will be fine.'

By the time they had sailed out to the island, it was almost dark, and a bitter drizzling mist was falling. 'I'm cold,' said Gareth.

'Alright,' said Hamish. 'We'll light a wee fire tah keep yee warm.'

Soon after lighting the fire, they heard something slapping against the wet rocks. There, coming toward them, was a group of strange creatures, half human and half seal. As they came closer, the boys could see that they were *selkies* coming ashore for the night, shedding their sealskins and changing into human form.

'I'm scared!' exclaimed Gareth. Hamish motioned for his younger brother to get behind him. Suddenly, a big, strong selkie came forward, swinging a club. 'We know what yer up to! Yee came here tah kill us so yee can have all the fish tah yourselves!'

An ancient selkie stepped in front of the younger one, leaning on a gnarly driftwood cane. His long beard looked like sea moss blowing in the wind. 'Duh nee harm a hair on their heads!' he cried.

'But why, Grandfather?' asked the young selkie.

'Because if it weren't for the father of these boys, I'd nee be alive tahday, and neither would you. Back when I was your age, I was caught in a fisherman's net, and nearly drowned. When the fisherman found me in his net, he cut me free and destroyed it. That fisherman was the father of these boys, and he saved me life.' Then the old selkie turned toward Hamish and his brothers. 'Boys, we know what yee came here tah do, and we shouldn't let yee leave here alive. But I'm goin' tah give yah one chance to live, in gratitude tah your father for savin' me life. Then my debt will be paid. Yah better hurry and leave now, before I change me mind!'

Hamish and his two brothers ran toward their boat, slipping and stumbling on the seaweed-covered rocks as they went. The seal folk parted to let them pass. When they reached the boat, Hamish didn't even take the time to set the sails. He slipped the oars into their locks and rowed as fast as he could all the way home. When they finally stepped out of the boat, Hamish, still shaking, caught his breath, turned toward his two brothers, and said, 'Not a word tah Dah about this, boys. When we get tah the house, go right tah bed and duh nee say a thing. Do yah hear me?'

'Aye,' they said in unison.

When the boys walked through the door, their father was sitting and reading the Good Book. He lowered his spectacles, looked at the boys, and asked, 'Hamish? Boys? Where have yee been?'

'Oh, those nets were in a terrible way,' Hamish replied. 'Aye, they needed a lot ah work.'

Their father thought for a moment, then said, 'Alright, boys. Off tah bed with yah.'

'G'night, Dah.'

'Goodnight, boys.'"

~

AFTER ABBY HAD FINISHED telling the story, it lingered in the salty breeze blowing between them. Chris wondered what she was trying to tell him. He waited for some time, and then ventured, "Abby?"

"Why do people always want more?" she wondered. "Why is it never enough? To us, it's a meal or a sport, but to them, it's their life."

Chris was taken aback. After all the trauma and pain that Abigail had been through, she was still thinking about the animals she'd fought so hard to protect. He also sensed that she was not posing the question to him, but instead probing her own mind for the answer. He wondered about this as he studied her profile. Her wild, windblown hair mirrored the roiling emotions that flowed between them. Abby didn't turn to face him. She kept her eyes on the seaward horizon. "I don't know, Abby. Perhaps it's just human nature to never be satisfied with what we have."

Abby didn't respond at first. When she finally turned to face him, he could see the anger in her eyes. "Yes," she said. "You ought to know." Then she walked past him, making her way down the declivity of the dune and backtracking along the trail toward the cottage, Chris trailing close behind.

44

Fiorelli was working in her office, finally wrapping up the paperwork and evidence for the Artemisian case. She was eager to get this final piece of the work behind her. Her phone buzzed, and Chief Morales called her into his office.

"Fiorelli, have a seat. How's that big case wrapping up?"

"The details are critical, but not my favorite part of the work, as you know. And I'm still having a hard time concentrating after everything that's happened."

"Your work on this case was extraordinary. You have a way of making connections by finding the finest threads of evidence and weaving them together like no detective I've ever worked with. It took your unique skill set and years of experience to solve that case."

"Thank you, Chief. I appreciate that."

"And your eye for detail, and knowledge of what might otherwise seem like an unconnected set of trivial facts…it's like nothing I've ever seen."

"Chief…what…?"

"Abby, that is why I called you in here. Here's what I'd like you to do. Once you've wrapped up this case—dotted all the i's and crossed the t's—take some time to collect yourself. You'll be more effective after you've had a chance to process what just happened and get some much-deserved rest and recuperation. You need time to heal. That case was one of the most intense we've ever had in this agency, and the details were…well…disturbing, to say the least. Let me leave it at that."

"Now you're reading my mind. I could really use a long break from work right now. And I need to get away from all the media attention and requests for interviews."

"That's exactly where I was going with this, Fiorelli. I'm glad we're on the same page."

"Is a month too long?"

"Are you kidding? With the untaken sick leave, overtime, and comp time you've clocked, the number crunchers are going to be on both our cases pretty soon if you don't take some serious time off."

45

Chris and Rhonda sat together on a beach blanket, looking out at the perfect day on Coast Guard Beach. Rafts of seals were bobbing offshore, seemingly oblivious to the people swimming nearby. Swells were rolling in at just the right height for body surfing. Bouncing up and down in the waves were Abby, Tommy, Piper, and Alicia.

Chris gazed out at the four of them. Watching the red highlights in Abby's thick head of hair fluttering in the midday sun, Chris noticed that at any given time, the three children would encircle their Aunt Abigail like planets revolving around a star. And he could see what was drawing them in. Her love for them was like gravity holding their little solar system together.

"This is the first time I've seen Abby enjoying herself since the Artemisians," observed Chris. "It's so good to see her laughing."

"I have to admit, I was really worried about hah," said Rhonda. "Whenevah she finishes a hahd case, she often needs time to figyah it out. But it's nevah been anythin' like it was this time. I think she's doin' some real soul-searchin'. I hope she finds the ansahs that she's lookin' faw. And speakin' of soul searchin', Chris...I've been meanin' tah ask yah."

"What's that, Rhonda?"

"Have Abby and yahself worked things out ovah the feelins she had about when yah was absent while she was in the hospital? She hasn't said very much about it, but I know it hurt hah deeply."

Chris paused for a time before answering. "I told her how sorry I am, and explained to her how twisted up my mind became when she was injured. Can you imagine being so afraid of losing someone you love that the pain from that feeling could make you ask yourself whether you can go on?"

"How do you think I feel when Mahk leaves for work every day? One stray bullet, and ah lives could change forevah. It's the hahdest thing I deal with in my life. I've learned to live with it, but it's nevah fah from my thoughts. But look out theyah, Chris," she said, pointing to the children out in the water with Abby. "I'd walk through any kind of emotional pain faw them. I'd walk through fiyah, and not regret a single minute of it."

"You really are an amazing person, Rhonda. Did you know that? I think Abby's heard what I went through, and even understands to a certain degree. But once she started recovering from her injuries—the emotional and the physical—the anger she felt toward me started to come out. Not so much directly, but in holding herself emotionally distant. I don't think that is going to change until I can regain her trust. And I pray to God that she gives me a lifetime to do just that."

Rhonda turned away from watching the children and looked directly at Chris. "Have yah told hah what yah just said tah me?"

"Not yet. I've been waiting until she's been able to heal and find her bearings before…you know.…"

"Yeah, I know. And I also know that such a commitment would, to a woman who loves someone, be just the kind of promise that could heal things and grow a sense of trust. Yah'll have tah trust me on this, Chris. And believe me, as much as I think the world of yah, my loyalty is to Abby. If I didn't think yah was made faw each othah, and that yah could make hah happy, I wouldn't even be sittin' heah talkin' to yah like this."

"I hear you, Rhonda. I don't think I've ever said this, but I think that in the ways of the human heart, you are one of the wisest people I've ever met."

"Then prove what yah said is true. But only do it if yah love Abby with all of yah haht, and ah willing to make that kind of commitment to hah."

～

AFTER ABBY AND THE children became accustomed to the cool water and their excitement at finally getting to swim in the ocean this summer had settled down, Chris noticed that they all turned to face the sea, watching and waiting to catch the next big wave and ride it to shore. The four of them stood patiently, jumping up every time a smaller wave passed by. Finally, off in the distance, he could see a big one rolling in. When the perfect wave finally arrived, everyone leapt toward shore to try and catch the crest, but only Tommy and Abby were able to hold the ride all the way in.

When the wave played out and the group stood up together, Chris noticed Tommy's expression as he addressed Abby, and the way he was looking at her. Keeping his eyes upon them, he said to Rhonda, "Tommy has a crush on Abby."

"No way! Do yah think?" She nudged him with her shoulder to signal that she already knew.

"So, you've noticed, too? The way he looks at her and acts when he's around her. He's smitten."

"But he's only twelve."

"Don't underestimate the feelings of a boy on the verge of adolescence. Heck, the first big crush I can remember was my fourth-grade teacher, Miss. Hall. She, too, was tall, and super nice to all the students. I remember one day, a stray dog got onto the schoolyard and was chasing and snapping at the students."

"What happened?"

The dog came after Miss Hall and I pulled it off of her, but it bit right through the skin of my hand. The injury wasn't that bad, but there was a lot of blood, and I ended up getting so much gratitude and attention from Miss Hall that I didn't feel a thing."

"And yah point is?"

"I see that same look on Tommy's face. In his eyes, Abby isn't surfing the waves, she's walking on water. He would do anything for her."

Abby and the children turned and headed in the direction of the beach blanket. Watching Abby with the children, Chris was reminded that her grace was a natural part of who she was, not a self-conscious affectation as it was with some attractive women. As Abby walked along the sand, every set of male eyes followed her movement. Chris noticed that quite a few of the women were watching her, as well. He knew that it was because of her beauty and the way she carried herself, but he was also aware that the unwanted renown arriving in the aftermath of the Artemisian case had made her a reluctant celebrity. For Abby—someone who had spent a lifetime trying to do good work in the world without drawing attention to herself—the newfound fame was a burden and a struggle.

When the group reached the blankets, Rhonda brushed Tommy's hair with her hand, and he ducked his head to shake her off because he didn't want to look like mama's little boy in front of Abby. Rhonda caught a look in Chris's eyes that seemed to say *I told you so*, and she shook her head at him as if to say *men are all the same!*

Abby and Chris moved to the beach towel furthest from Rhonda and the children. He leaned into her ear and whispered, "Every man on this beach is tracking your every move, hoping in vain for something they'll never have."

"It's not my fault. I knew we were coming with the kids,

so I wore this bottom with the little skirt on it. See?" she said in frustration. "This is why I don't go to the beach very often."

"Abby, wearing that bottom only leaves more to the imagination."

She whacked him on the shoulder. "Stop it. This is a family outing, not some *Beach Blanket Bingo* movie, and I'm not Sophia Loren."

"So, first off, it was Annette Funicello in *Beach Blanket Bingo*, not Sophia Loren."

"I know. I'm just testing you."

"And even if both of them were here, you'd put them to shame."

"Not."

They both smiled, and Abby finally leaned into Chris, pushing him playfully with her shoulder. "Keep talking. Don't let me interrupt."

Chris whispered again in her ear. "In all honesty, Abby, if I ever told you how much I love to look at you, and how often I wish we were off alone making love someplace, you'd be amazed."

"Talk is easy."

"I'll deal with you when we get back to your place."

"Promises, promises," Abby replied, putting her head on his shoulder and interlacing her fingers with his.

Epilogue

Fiorelli stepped out of the shower and walked into the living room wearing nothing but a towel. Chris looked up from his newspaper. "Do you require my assistance with something? Because you know, I'm always here for you."

"I'll bet you say that to all the half-naked women you see."

"No need to when I've got you."

"Boy, you're really working it today, buddy."

"I can't help it. You always get me going, but there's something about you when you've just solved a case that I find really attractive."

"I'll bet it's my high moral character."

"Not exactly. And I'm not kidding."

"Then what?"

"I know this case has been different from any other, but normally, you have a kind of glow around you at those times. It's hard to explain. It's like you've accomplished something you know you were put on this Earth to do."

"How did we go so quickly from physical attraction to philosophy? If that's where we're headed, I can think of a few more things I want to do with my life while there's still time."

"This is something new."

"New for us, perhaps, but not new for me. And as you said, this case was different. I don't think things are ever going to be quite the same. The experience shifted something inside of me, and it's going to take some time to figure out just what that means for the future."

"I want to explore this further, Abby. But aren't you hungry?"

"Not for food. Maybe some wine?"

The two of them sat side by side on the couch, sipping a rich merlot. After a few minutes, they spoke at the same time.

"Is there something...?" started Chris.

"I've been thinking...." said Fiorelli. She took Chris' hand. Out of the blue, she pronounced, "The chief gave me some orders last week."

"Really? I thought he pretty much let you follow your own instincts on these cases."

"That's true. But it wasn't that."

"Then what?"

"He ordered me to take some time off."

"Really?"

"When are you going to be done grading exams from your summer courses?" Abby asked.

"In about a week. Why, what are you scheming up?"

"Well, you know where I've been wanting to go for a long time?"

"Prince Edward Island?" Chris asked reflexively.

"Yes. The birds start gathering for migration very early that far north, even in late August."

"I've heard that birding on the islands in the Maritimes is amazing. Is this a proposition?"

"An invitation."

"Count me in. And Abby?"

"Yes."

"There's something I've been meaning to ask you."

Afterword

Detective Fiorelli's World and
the Plight of Endangered Species

EYE OF THE OCELOT is a work of fiction, as are all of the characters who breathe life into the narrative. The geography and natural history of Cape Cod and the wider world, however, are factual and true. The plants and animals animating the wild realms of Abigail Fiorelli's world, and the habitats where they live, appear just as readers will find them on their next excursion to the remarkably diverse environments on the Cape.

Abigail Fiorelli has a love for all wild things nurtured by long nature walks in childhood with her late mother, Fiona—memories she cherishes dearly. In *Eye of the Ocelot*, Fiorelli's love of animals is the driving force behind her indomitable pursuit of the Artemisians and their depraved use of endangered species for rituals based upon myth and superstition. Fiorelli is passionate about the cause, and relentless in her pursuit of the perpetrators.

As naturalists and biologists, Fiorelli and her beau, Chris Armstrong, are intimately acquainted with the value of each plant and animal species as well as the irreplaceable richness they afford our world. Each species in the ecosystem—and the biological and genetic diversity encoded in its DNA—is unique in all the world. Pull out one thread in the fabric of life, and it begins to fray. Pull too many threads, and the weave unravels.

Ecosystems determine the lives of plants and animals, and they, in turn, shape their own environments. This includes human beings. What would the history and cultures of Indigenous peoples be without the winged icons of eagles and condors, or totems of bison and salmon? Our aesthetic experience of nature is intricately linked to its spiritual and inspirational influence upon our lives, affirming our sense of what it really means for the world we inhabit to be right and whole.

Alas, it cannot be said that the criminal trade of endangered species and their parts is a work of fiction. Detective Fiorelli's concerns are more than well-founded. While *Eye of the Ocelot* depicts extreme exploitation of endangered species, it also reflects craven illegal activities that are only too real in today's world.

Trafficking of endangered species is a global phenomenon. Endangered species and their parts are used for everything from food and lumber to boutique clothing, *objets d'art*, and knick-knacks. They're also used for medication and aphrodisiacs—the efficacy of which has been disproven. Illegal hunting and poaching have driven thousands of rare species to the brink of extinction. Many plants and animals have been wiped out entirely—and eternally.

Since 1964, the International Union for Conservation

of Nature (IUCN) has maintained the global Red List of Threatened Species as a means of measuring the health of Earth's declining biodiversity. As of this writing, the IUCN Red List contains 32,000 species threatened by extinction, "...including 41% of amphibians, 34% of conifers, 33% of reef-building corals, 26% of mammals, and 14% of birds" (www.iucnredlist.org).

Most people are aware of the heinous practices of poaching elephants for their ivory tusks and killing rhinoceroses solely for their horns. Few, however, are aware of the plight of thousands of unheralded, lesser-known endangered animals: Cuba's solenodon, the Mediterranean monk seal, the Amazon river dolphin, Italy's amphibious olm, New Zealand's Kakapos parrot, the humphead wrasse of the Pacific and Indian Oceans, North America's cobblestone tiger beetle, Asia's lesser panda, the Philippine eagle, and Australia's Tasmanian devil.

The Convention on International Trade in Endangered Species of Wild Fauna and Flora (CITES) was formed in the 1960s as an agreement between international governments to monitor and regulate international trade in endangered species to ensure their survival. Every year, billions of dollars are exchanged for hundreds of millions of endangered plants and animals and their parts, from furs and pelts to lumber and seeds. There are currently 183 parties to the CITES international agreement, ranging from the United States (the first nation to join, in 1974) to the most recent signatory (Tonga, in 2016).

The CITES international agreement aims to protect and ensure the survival of over 37,000 species of live plants, animals, and fungi, and expressly forbids the use of their parts for any purpose. With few exceptions, only habitat destruction is considered to have a greater overall impact than poaching on the survival of threatened and endangered species around the globe. In addition, shifts in habitat and weather due to climate change now threaten thousands of species already stressed by the vicissitudes encountered by inhabitants of polar, alpine, and other extreme environments in our changing world. Additional threats imperiling plants and animals include invasive species, water pollution, human waste discarded on land and in oceans (especially plastic), and stressors brought about by an ever-increasing human population.

What is the current status of the endangered animals on the menu during the Artemisians' twisted ritual meal?

The **ocelot** (*Leopardus pardalis*) is a lithe, elegantly-marked wild cat that can weigh up to 33 pounds (15 kg). It grows up to 40 inches (101 cm) long, and its tail can reach 20 inches (50 cm). Leopard-like markings, set in a soft, smooth coat of yellow-brown to reddish-gray fur, run the length of its body. Its white belly is speckled with black spots, and its tail is ringed with a black tip.

Ocelots inhabit a range from South Texas to Central America and the northern half of South America, but they are declining. Because they are listed as endangered under the United States Endangered Species Act, it is against the law in the United States (EPA) and worldwide (CITES) to harm ocelots. All trade is illegal. The ocelot's survival is threatened by habitat destruction and fragmentation due to agriculture, development, and road construction. Many ocelots succumb to vehicle strikes, poaching for pets and furs, and programs aimed at killing coyotes, bobcats, bears, and other wild animals to protect cattle. Barriers across the United States border with Mexico restrict the movement of ocelots between the two countries, resulting in genetically isolated populations.

Rhinoceroses were once found in Africa, Asia, and Europe. Of their five species, some have two horns, while others have one. They have been hunted mercilessly for their horns, which are then ground up and used as a traditional Chinese medicine—falsely reputed to serve as an aphrodisiac and treatment for various ailments. From the beginning of the 20th century through the present, the total number of rhinos in the world dropped from half a million to less than 30,000.

In Africa, the western black rhino and northern white rhino have been extirpated in the wild; of the latter, there remain only two captive individuals in the world. Javan rhinos and Sumatran rhinos are critically endangered, with less than 100 individuals left. Greater one-horned rhinos are vulnerable to endangerment if trends do not change. Southern white rhinos are vulnerable, but their population has been increasing.

The **California condor** (*Gymnogyps californianus*) can

weigh more than 20 pounds and is the largest bird in North America. With a wingspan of up to 9.5 feet, condors can stay aloft for hours without flapping their wings. They can fly 150 miles in one day searching for food, soar at over 55 miles per hour, and ride the winds up to 15,000 feet.

Condors live in hilly and mountainous places with rocky, forested slopes, gorges, and canyons. Excellent eyesight enables them to see long distances when searching for food, which consists mostly of the decaying remains of animals both large and small. Their naked head helps them to stay clean when feeding on carrion.

Although they can live for more than 40 years, the California condor's mating cycle and behavior make it extremely vulnerable as a species. They don't start to reproduce until six to seven years of age. Eggs take nearly two months to hatch, and adults (both parents) need to take care of the chicks and young for more than six months.

For 40,000 years, condors soared across a vast range that we identify today as California and the other Pacific states; north to British Columbia; south to Baja California; and east as far as Texas, Florida, and New York. Over time, humans came perilously close to exterminating this magnificent species by shooting them, poisoning their food, capturing them, collecting and eating their eggs, and killing their primary food sources (for example, elk and antelope). Reproduction was also severely decreased by exposure to environmental toxins such as the pesticide DDT, in addition to lead, which was ingested via ammunition found in the remains of animals. By 1982, the California condor had been designated a critically endangered species. With only 22 condors left in the world, the species was on the brink of extinction.

To save the remaining condors, biologists captured all of the surviving wild birds in order to protect them and increase their numbers through captive breeding. There were none left in the wild between 1988 and 1991, when they were again reintroduced into their natural environment. With the assistance of wildlife biologists and conservationists, and with regulations in place controlling the release of toxins into the environment, condor numbers had increased to over 500 by early 2022.

Wind power turbines now pose a new threat to the survival of condors. Still, there are now some 181 condors living in captivity, and 337 in the wild. They are found flying free in Southern California and in the Central Coast region, as well as in Arizona, Utah, and Baja, Mexico. Plans are now underway to reintroduce condors to the traditional tribal lands of the Yurok at the mouth of the Klamath River, where it flows into the Pacific Ocean in northern California.

Grizzly bears (*Ursus arctos horribilis*) are 800-pound, eight-foot-tall giants that fear only one predator: human beings. Populations of these magnificent animals dropped precipitously throughout North America in the aftermath of European settlement. Grizzlies were wiped out across vast regions of Canada, including Saskatchewan, Manitoba, and large portions of Labrador and northern Québec. About three-fourths of the remaining Canadian populations of grizzlies live in Yukon and British Columbia. They are also found in Nunavut, Alberta, and the Northwest Territories.

In the United States, however, grizzlies have been on the endangered species list since 1975. Prior to that year, they were wiped out across most of their habitat in the lower 48 states, chiefly because of the federal government's predator control program. Grizzles are now found in less than two percent of the range they once occupied. According to the Center for Biological Diversity, the five areas of the United States where grizzlies now live encompass the Greater Yellowstone ecosystem (including Yellowstone National Park); the Northern Continental Divide ecosystem (including Glacier National Park); the Northern Cascades in Washington; the Selkirks in northern Idaho; and the Cabinet-Yaak in northeastern Idaho and northwestern Montana.

Endangered Species Recovery

Each of us, in our own way, can become involved in saving endangered species from extinction. Conservation and recovery efforts have led to the resurgence of the bald eagle, a gradual increase in the number of grizzly bears, and the slow rise of near-extinct species like Asia's greater one-horned (Indian) rhinoceros, whose numbers have risen from about 200 in 1900 to over 3,700 today. Due to habitat preservation, restoration, and bans on hunting, poaching, and toxic environmental substances, many other species worldwide have been brought back from the brink of extinction, including the California condor, the humpback whale, the peregrine falcon, the Indian rhinoceros, the West Indian manatee, the green sea turtle, and the orangutan. In addition, the Kirtland's warbler—which Abigail Fiorelli's partner Chris Armstrong studied in graduate school—is now doing well as a result of habitat management and control of a nest parasite, the brown-headed cowbird.

What can you do to help protect threatened and endangered species?

- Never buy anything made from endangered species or their parts, or anything produced in a way that harms the environment in which endangered species live.

- Support organizations that work directly to save endangered species and their habitats, such as Earth Justice, Defenders of Wildlife, the Natural Resources Defense Council, the World Wildlife Fund, the National Wildlife Federation, the National Audubon Society, the Center for Biological Diversity, and Sea Shepherd. Get involved in your local conservation organizations and the National Endangered Species Coalition.

- Endangered species live everywhere. Find out about endangered species in your region. Support and get involved with local conservation organizations that work to protect and save local plants, animals, and habitats.

- Use less paper (wood), energy (fossil fuels), and, above all, plastic (oil). Drive less, use mass transportation whenever possible, and walk and bicycle more often. Simplifying our lifestyles and focusing on the essentials are systematic ways of lowering demand for materials that must be cut, mined, or pumped out of the ground—actions that degrade, destroy, and threaten habitats for all species while polluting the environments upon which they depend for survival.

- Reuse and recycle as much as possible of your household's waste stream to decrease demand on resources and related habitat destruction.

- Look for products made from recycled materials and resources that come from sustainably-managed operations like responsible forestry and agriculture.

- Reduce and eliminate the use of plastic wherever possible, including single-use plastic bags, straws, clamshell food containers, beverage bottles, and packaging. Alternatives include reusable grocery bags, glass and metal bottles, and refillable coffee cups and water bottles. Buy food in bulk, and support food merchants and restaurants that use paper-based food containers and reusable and biodegradable straws. From wild camels to dolphins, many endangered species mistake plastic for food. They ingest large quantities, filling their stomachs with material that can't be eliminated. As a result, they experience a slow decline in health, and will eventually suffer infection and starvation. The nearly

8 billion people in the world use some 300 million tons of plastic each year, 8 million tons of which end up in the ocean. Marine mammals become entangled in this plastic. It is estimated that 90 percent of all seabirds have some plastic in their stomachs.

• Spend more time out in nature—walking, bird-watching, and visiting natural areas to learn about the life around you. Support local environments through your interest and usage fees.

• Do things at home that make your environment safer for all species, like putting decals on windows near birdfeeders to prevent birds from being injured when they fly into glass. Keep domestic cats inside. Audubon estimates that each year, in the lower 48 states alone, cats kill 1.4 to 3.7 billion birds and 6.9 to 20.7 billion mammals (www.audubon.org).

• Use organic fertilizers, pesticides, and herbicides in your yard and garden. Minimize their application to avoid poisoning insects and other wildlife.

• Watch the road to avoid hitting crossing animals (while making sure to drive safely). If you see an animal starting to cross the road, beep your horn and slow down in a safe manner. Many animals don't know how to react to a moving car, but will turn and run away from traffic when confronted with the sound of a horn.

Can any of us really make a difference? Think of it as the *power of one*. Every individual action impacts the environment. And when millions or even billions of people are engaged, our cumulative actions exert a synergistic effect upon the world around us. For instance, if everyone on the planet stopped using plastic drinking straws, billions of dangerous plastic pieces would never be introduced into the environment, where they pose a significant threat to wildlife and endangered species. There is a real reason Detective Fiorelli becomes a global phenomenon when people hear about the personal cost of her heroic efforts to stop the Artemisians from exploiting endangered animals: Individuals care deeply about other people and the wondrous forms of life with whom we share this beautiful planet.

Acknowledgments

FIRST AND FOREMOST, THANK you, the readers—who bring the story to life in your mind's eye.

Love and deepest thanks to my devoted partner, other family members, and friends who tolerated my intellectual and emotional absences while I was immersed in creating Abigail Fiorelli's world.

Sincere thanks and appreciation to Cathryn Lykes for lending her keen editorial eye and creative literary skills for the developmental and technical editing of the evolving manuscript (cathrynlykes.com).

As a lifelong student of nature, I wanted to ensure that the natural history presented in the manuscript was accurate and true to the specific locations on Cape Cod. For this review, I turned to a longstanding colleague with a laser eye for natural history, including inimate knowledge of the plants and animals on Cape Cod and all things avian. My sincere thanks to Dr. Walter Ellison, former Lecturer in Biology at Washington College in Chestertown, Maryland.

I am also grateful to Christine Horner, The Book Cover Whisperer, for creating the powerful and moving cover image and elegant interior design for the various book formats (openbookdesign.biz).

—Volta Rose